AN IVY HILL
CHRISTMAS

A TALES FROM IVY HILL NOVELLA

AN IVY HILL CHRISTMAS

JULIE KLASSEN

BETHANYHOUSE

a division of Baker Publishing Group
Minneapolis, Minnesota

© 2020 by Julie Klassen

Published by Bethany House Publishers
11400 Hampshire Avenue South
Bloomington, Minnesota 55438
www.bethanyhouse.com

Bethany House Publishers is a division of
Baker Publishing Group, Grand Rapids, Michigan

Printed in the United States of America

Library of Congress Cataloging-in-Publication Data
Names: Klassen, Julie, author.
Title: An Ivy Hill Christmas : a tales from Ivy Hill novella / Julie Klassen.
Description: Minneapolis, Minnesota : Bethany House Publishers, [2020] | Series: Tales from Ivy Hill ; 5
Identifiers: LCCN 2020011428 | ISBN 9780764233807 (trade paperback) | ISBN 9780764233814 (cloth) | ISBN 9780764236198 (large print) | ISBN 9781493425136 (ebook)
Subjects: GSAFD: Christian fiction. | Love stories.
Classification: LCC PS3611.L37 I98 2020 | DDC 813/.6—dc23
LC record available at https://lccn.loc.gov/2020011428

Scripture quotations are from the King James Version of the Bible.

Cover design by Jennifer Parker
Cover photography by Mike Habermann Photography, LLC
Map illustration by Bek Cruddace Cartography & Illustration

Author is represented by Books and Such Literary Agency.

20 21 22 23 24 25 26   7 6 5 4 3 2 1

To Michelle Griep,
talented writer of novels, novellas,
and spot-on critiques,
with love and gratitude.

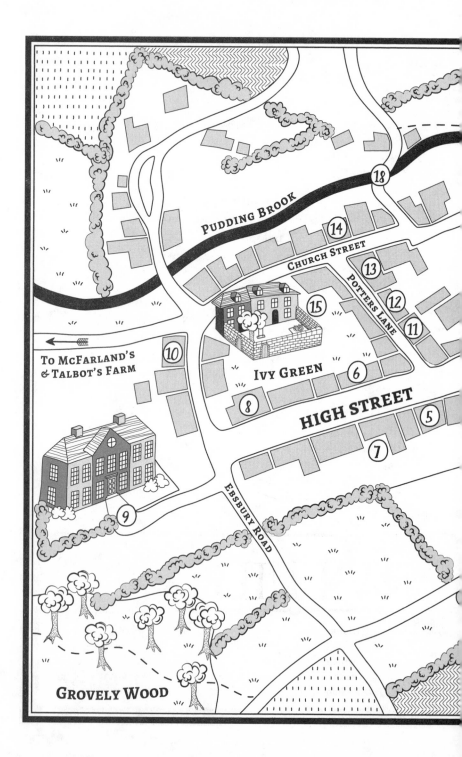

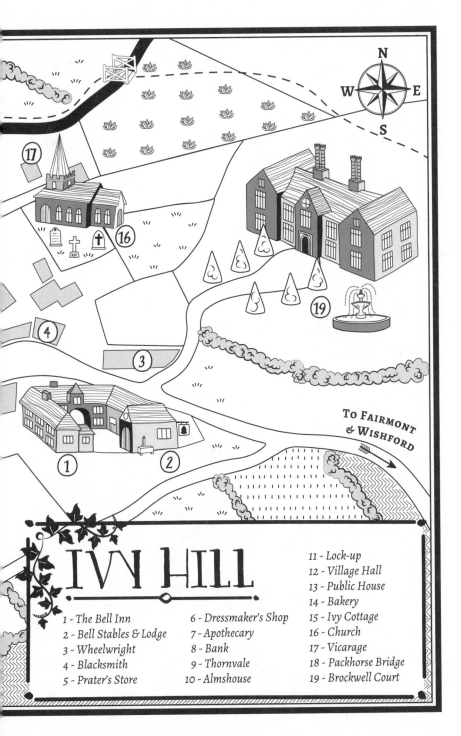

IVY HILL

1 - The Bell Inn
2 - Bell Stables & Lodge
3 - Wheelwright
4 - Blacksmith
5 - Prater's Store
6 - Dressmaker's Shop
7 - Apothecary
8 - Bank
9 - Thornvale
10 - Almshouse
11 - Lock-up
12 - Village Hall
13 - Public House
14 - Bakery
15 - Ivy Cottage
16 - Church
17 - Vicarage
18 - Packhorse Bridge
19 - Brockwell Court

To Fairmont & Wishford

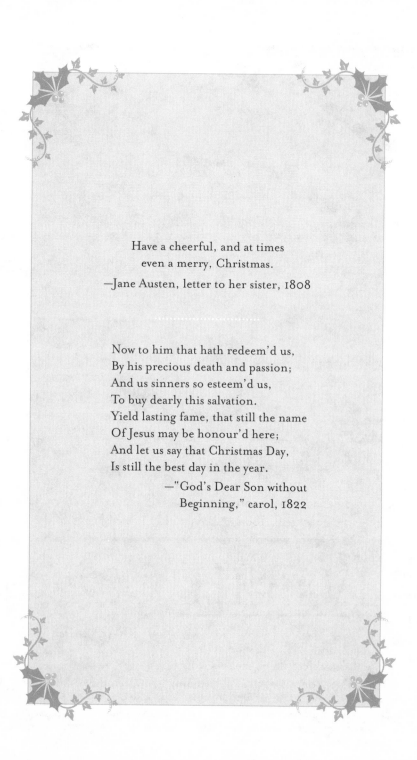

Have a cheerful, and at times
even a merry, Christmas.

—Jane Austen, letter to her sister, 1808

Now to him that hath redeem'd us,
By his precious death and passion;
And us sinners so esteem'd us,
To buy dearly this salvation.
Yield lasting fame, that still the name
Of Jesus may be honour'd here;
And let us say that Christmas Day,
Is still the best day in the year.

—"God's Dear Son without
Beginning," carol, 1822

December 1822
London

Walking past a linen draper's, Richard Brockwell surveyed his reflection in the shop windows with approval. He cut a fine figure, although he said it himself. Inside, he glimpsed a pretty debutante he had been introduced to at some ball or other. She had flirted with him, and they had danced once, but he had not asked her again nor called on her afterward. Nor did he stop to renew their acquaintance now. She was too young and too . . . eligible.

He walked on. A stern-looking older woman stood outside the humble chapel on the corner. In hopes of avoiding her, he crossed the cobbled street. Too late. Her voice gripped his neck like a mother cat grasping the scruff of her wayward offspring.

"You, sir! Will you make a donation to our most worthy charity?" Dodging a passing hackney coach, she strode across the street to accost him.

Richard turned and pasted on a smile. His upbringing, while not without its faults, had taught him to feign politeness with ease.

Reaching him, she went on with her appeal, "I am Miss Arbuthnot, directress of the St. George Orphan Refuge. We rescue orphans from the retreats of villainy and teach them skills like printing, bookbinding, and twine spinning to enable them to obtain an honest living." She held out a basket. "Our institution is supported by voluntary contributions."

Voluntary or coerced? Richard wondered. He warmly replied, "My dear madam, how I look forward to you or one of your comrades addressing me almost every time I pass this way. Your . . . stamina is breathtaking. You rival an athlete in a Greek pentathlon."

Her eyes narrowed, but he persisted with his most charming smile. "I applaud your philanthropic spirit. Truly. And like you, I give all I can spare to my charity of choice. My favorite coffeehouse and bookshop have first claim on my heart—and my purse."

With a pert bow, he turned and walked on, leaving her sputtering and him quite satisfied with himself.

Richard was, he knew, a selfish creature. A person could not change his nature, his very heart, could he? He thought not.

Reaching the coffeehouse, he tipped his hat to the beggar outside and entered the beloved establishment, the aromas of coffee, pipe tobacco, newsprint, and books rushing up to greet him. Seeing his bespectacled editor bent over a newspaper at their usual table, Richard walked over to join him.

"Murray. Good to see you, old boy."

David Murray raised his dark curly head and stood to shake Richard's hand. "How are you, Brockwell?"

"According to the papers, I am a handsome rake bent on seducing all the widows of Mayfair." He smirked at the exaggeration and sat down. At one time, he probably deserved his roguish reputation, but no longer.

"Better than my lot," Murray grumbled. "According to this morning's edition, I am about to be taken to court on charges of libel again and am on the verge of bankruptcy."

Richard grinned at his friend, only two years his senior. "Ah well, we each have our crosses to bear. Perhaps this will help." He extracted several sheets of paper from his leather portfolio. "Here is the article you asked for. I shall have to mail you the next piece from Wiltshire."

The man's bushy eyebrows rose over his spectacles. "Thought you planned to stay in Town and work through Christmas."

"I did, but my mother is insisting I come home this year. I dread it, but she is not taking no for an answer."

"Christmas surrounded by doting loved ones?" Murray said dryly. "Horrors."

His editor had no family, Richard knew. An idea struck him. The distraction of an unexpected houseguest might come in handy. "Why don't you come with me? That is, if you can bear the thought of Christmas in the country?"

"When do you leave?"

"On the nineteenth."

The man hesitated. "You go on, but I trust you will submit a new piece of scathing satire by the tenth of next month, as usual? Or will the comforts of Christmas in the country addle your brains and make you soft?"

"Never. But perhaps you had better come along to make sure I keep my wits about me."

He did not tell his friend that he was also working on a second novel. The first had already been rejected by two publishers. In fact, Thomas Cadell, of the eminent London publishing firm Cadell & Davies, sent only a curt, *Declined by Return of Post*. Richard was still awaiting a reply from a third and fourth firm. Unfortunately Murray did not publish books, preferring to focus on his magazine.

"Would your family not mind a houseguest?" Murray asked.

"Not at all. They always invite guests at Christmas."

"May I have a day or two to think about it?"

"Of course. Just let me know when you decide."

Richard himself spent as little time at Brockwell Court as possible, preferring to live in the family's London townhouse, away from his mother's matchmaking schemes and the guilt of knowing he had disappointed her yet again. For all intents and purposes, he was the master of the fine London residence with its small, efficient staff.

He gladly left the responsibilities of the country estate to his older brother, dutiful Sir Timothy. And why not? He was heir after all, and not him.

Richard had no desire to travel to rural Wiltshire, attend church services and parties, politely greet people he barely remembered, and listen to his widowed mother's doleful sighs. The dowager Lady Brockwell had always been somber and reserved, though perhaps now that Timothy and his pretty wife had their first child, she would cheer up and leave off pressuring him to marry.

And Richard *would* enjoy spending time with his younger sister, Justina. Hosting her for a London season had been a real pleasure. In Justina's eyes, he could do no wrong, and he had relished her youthful adoration and easy laughter at his jokes. Shepherding her through the season had also funneled more money into their London accounts, which he had not minded at all. Money that was sadly long gone.

Thankfully, his mother had always been persuadable where money was concerned and would write to the bankers to advance more funds whenever he asked.

Until now.

Now she was taking a hard line, insisting there would be no more bank drafts, at least until he came home for Christmas.

That evening, Richard sat down to a dinner of roast beef and potatoes. He eyed his half glass of claret with displeasure, then raised it toward Pickering.

"That's the last of it, sir," replied his aging valet who also waited at table. "And there's no money for more."

Richard sighed and shifted his focus outside.

The evening had turned dark, and a storm descended, matching his mood. Rain pelted the French doors while branches of a nearby shrub, propelled by the wind, lashed its panes.

Lightning flashed, illuminating a pair of eyes beyond the glass. Curious, Richard rose and looked closer. A bedraggled dog sat outside the door. Noticing Richard, the pathetic creature rose on short hind legs and placed its paws on the glass. Eyes large and pleading, he looked longingly at Richard's snug room and warm fire—or perhaps simply at his plate of roast beef.

Another flash of lightning. And in that flash, Richard saw himself as a boy, standing all alone at a cottage window, staring at a scene of comfort—an outsider looking in, wanting to belong. To be loved and accepted.

"Ignore it, sir," Pickering said dully, "and it will go away."

Richard rose and went to the door. "Let's feed it something at least."

The elderly man shook his head. "I am not going out in that. Besides, if you feed a stray, you'll never get rid of it."

Well Richard knew. But rare pity stirred in his heart. He unlatched and opened the door, then cajoled the skittish dog inside with a soothing voice and piece of beef.

Pickering shook his head. "Mrs. Tompkins won't like it. She's struggling to make do with a sparse larder as it is."

He knew Pickering was right, but he did it anyway.

A week later, Richard prepared for the dreaded journey to Ivy Hill. At least Christmastide in the country would be more festive than in Town, he consoled himself, with good meals and access to Brockwell Court's well-stocked wine cellar. It was only a few weeks. He would make the most of it.

But when the festivities were over and the Twelfth Night cake eaten, he would be back on a coach bound for London and his unencumbered bachelor life.

He viewed his reflection in the mirror and then slipped a small waistcoat around his dog. His dour valet refused to do so.

"Bad enough dressing one young dandy," Pickering said. "Dressing that rascal is beneath even my dignity."

"Very well, you old curmudgeon. I shall do it myself." And he proceeded to button the waistcoat and tie a miniature cravat around the dog's neck, all reluctantly made by his own tailor.

Richard already liked the dog a vast deal more than he liked Pickering. More than most people, actually.

Although the dog's pedigree was doubtful, he reminded Richard of the terriers in *Guy Mannering*. In the novel, a Scottish farmer named Dandie Dinmont owned six "pepper and mustard" terriers as tough and friendly as he. Richard had thought of naming the stray Scotty, but that had seemed too obvious. He called him Wally instead, in begrudging honor of Sir Walter Scott. Most in the publishing world believed him to be the novel's author, though the printed attribution read only *By the author of Waverley*. *Guy Mannering* had sold out in its first twenty-four hours. Oh, to have even a tiny morsel of that author's success.

Instead, he had Wally. Already the dog was earning his keep. First, he'd cleared the cellar of mice, which won over Richard's cook-housekeeper. Second, attired in miniature clothes that matched his own, the dapper canine drew admiration wherever they went.

Today, Richard, Pickering, and Wally were bound for Wiltshire. Murray had decided to go along and would meet them at the coaching inn.

Wally looked dashing in his green coat, his fluffy fawn-and-ginger hair freshly bathed for the journey. The housemaid had ended up soaked afterward. He'd thought of giving her an extra crown for her trouble but had too few coins in his purse as it was.

Since Wally was small enough to sit on his lap, Richard had not even had to purchase a second seat for him inside the coach. Mr. Murray had bought his own. And to Richard's surprise, his old valet had bought himself an inside seat instead of a less expensive one outside.

"The wages you give me are poor indeed, but *I* am not," Pickering said, nose in the air. "Unlike you, Master Richard, I don't spend every farthing I receive while still warm from its giver."

"Well, bravo for you."

Pickering had been valet to Richard's father and, after Sir Justin's death, had joined him in London. He was likely the only man willing to serve at the outdated wages Richard's limited budget allowed. "Serve" might be an overstatement. At least Pickering enjoyed the free room and board, even if the wages were substandard. Probably stayed out of loyalty to his old sainted master. Richard felt his lip curl at the thought. Saint Sir Justin. What a laugh. He alone knew better.

Little relishing the old man's crusty comments, and knowing his mother would assign a footman to attend him, Richard had not asked Pickering to travel to Brockwell Court with them. But the annoying man had invited himself along anyway.

He'd said, "I have not been home for Christmas in years. I shan't miss my chance now. Who knows when my inconsiderate master will go again?"

Richard had smirked at the derisive comment but let it pass. Sincerely curious, he asked, "Do you still consider Ivy Hill home, Pickering? You have been in London with me for the better part of ten years."

"You need not remind me," the man said dryly. "As it happens, I grew up there and still have two nieces there, so yes, I will always consider it my home."

Richard shook his head. "London is my home."

He had also been a little surprised at Mrs. Tompkins's pleasure when he announced his upcoming departure. The cook-housekeeper had pressed him to give their small clutch of servants time off at Christmas to spend with their families. He had reluctantly agreed.

If he had not, he might have left Wally in the townhouse under the care of the housemaid or Billy, the general odd-job boy. Instead, he was taking the dog with him to Brockwell Court. Oh well. Wally's company would be worth the minor inconvenience of having to walk him every time they stopped to change horses. Besides, his mother's pampered pug was due for a setdown.

When the coach arrived at the London inn, they took their seats. As they waited for the baggage to be stowed and the coachman to make his final preparations, Richard looked out the window and noticed an elderly father in the courtyard bidding his grown son a fond farewell with an affectionate embrace.

Beside him, Murray mumbled, "What would that be like?"

No idea, Richard thought. Instead, he quipped, "Families exist to embarrass you. Be glad you're on your own."

Murray sent him a sidelong glance. "You don't fool me."

Surprise flashed through Richard. "I don't? Then I had better improve my game."

The coach was heavy-laden with Christmas travelers, parcels, geese, and several bluecoat schoolboys on the rooftop seats, on their way home for the holidays. An elderly matron took the final inside seat, a basket on her lap. Pickering tipped his hat to her, and Wally sniffed her basket with interest.

Soon they were rattling along cobbled streets and leaving the city behind. As the coach rumbled down the open road, Richard opened his leather portfolio and, with a pencil, began revising a chapter of his second novel. But his eyelids soon grew heavy. He gazed drowsily at the passing countryside and was about to nod off when a small body fell past his window. One of the rooftop passengers went tumbling to the ground. Wally barked an alarm.

Before he could react, Mr. Murray grabbed Richard's walking stick and pounded on the roof. "Stop! Stop the coach!"

"Careful—that's ivory," Richard gently chastised.

The coachman halted the horses, cursing the delay, and Murray stepped over the legs of the woman and Richard to see if he could help. He returned with a boy of about twelve who had a goose egg on his head but was otherwise remarkably unscathed.

Murray helped the lad inside. "Here, you take my seat and rest. I'll sit on the roof."

"Th-thank you, sir," the boy mumbled, looking a little dazed.

Richard secretly admired his friend's gesture . . . and his flannel-lined greatcoat. He would not give up his seat for a stranger. Not in such chilly, damp weather. With an apologetic glance at his shivery little dog, he justified, "Wally here would catch cold."

Pickering rolled his eyes. "Right."

The woman spoke in soothing tones to the boy and shared an apple and cheese with him from her basket. Richard was impressed by her selfless act as well. He might have shared his provisions, but neither the lad nor Wally would appreciate an offer to share the dog's food, which was all he had.

He studied the injured youth seated across from him—not one of the bluecoat boys, he realized, but rather a lad dressed in dark coat and trousers, grass-stained and dirty from his fall, with a flat wool cap on his head.

Out of sheer boredom, Richard struck up a conversation with him.

"Traveling alone?"

The lad shot him an uneasy glance. Such a wary, world-wise look for one so young.

Richard changed tack, turning his attention to the dog. "Wally and I are headed home for Christmas. How about you?"

The boy shook his head.

"No? You're a wiser man than I."

Wally strained in Richard's grasp, leaning eagerly toward the boy.

"He wants to come over and greet you. Do you mind?"

"No, sir. I like dogs."

Richard released him. Wally jumped up on the boy's lap and licked his cheek. Too bad he didn't lick the kid's runny nose while he was at it. With a regretful look at his pristine handkerchief, Richard handed it to the boy with a significant tap to his own nose.

The lad wiped with gusto, then handed it back.

Richard waved the offer away. "Keep it. An early Christmas present."

He'd said it in jest, but the boy beamed. "Thank you, sir!"

"What is your name?" Richard asked.

"Jamie Fleming."

"And where are you off to today?"

The lad told him he was on his way to begin an apprenticeship to a printer in Wiltshire—a commitment of seven years.

Richard raised his chin. "So you're to be a printer's devil, ey?"

"Yes, sir. Or so I've been told."

"Don't worry. I am often called a devil myself. You'll get used to it. Where is this printer?"

"Wishford, near Salisbury."

"Ah. I know it. Very near where my family lives."

Hope shone on the young face. "Then perhaps I shall see you sometime."

Richard hesitated. "It is possible. Now, no more falling off coaches, and I wish you every success in your future."

The boy's eyes dimmed. "Yes, sir."

The old woman leaned forward, brow furrowed. "Your parents must have been sorry to see you go, especially so near Christmas."

Jamie shook his head. "No, ma'am." He looked away. Petting the dog, he murmured, "My parents are both gone."

"I am sorry to hear it."

After a respectful moment of silence, Richard asked, "I'm curious. What does an apprenticeship cost these days?"

"Twenty pounds."

"Good night. How did you manage it?"

"The St. George Orphan Refuge paid the fee and my coach fare too. Have you heard of them?"

Richard answered dryly, "I am somewhat familiar with that institution, yes. They often ask me for money."

Earnestly, the boy said, "Then, I have you to thank as well."

"Heavens no. Don't thank me," Richard hurried to reply.

Pickering's wiry eyebrows rose. "You, sir? I didn't take you for a philanthropist."

"I am not. I said they asked. Never said I agreed."

After that, Richard lapsed into silence, provoked by this turn of events. That an orphan from that woman's charity would be seated across from him? Was some ironic fate at work here . . . or God? A shiver passed over him. *Only the cold*, he told himself and forced his attention back to his book.

CHAPTER
Two

Lady Brockwell, formerly Miss Rachel Ashford, kissed her husband and straightened his cravat. "Come, my dear. We don't want to be late for dinner and annoy your mother."

"You are the lady of the house now, my love, and the woman whose happiness I am most interested in."

"I know. Yet I do hope Richard does not disappoint her again." Sir Timothy kissed her cheek. "So do I."

They went downstairs and joined the other family members gathered in the drawing room: Lady Barbara and Justina.

No Richard.

The dowager lifted her pointy chin. "It is as I expected. He has defied me yet again. But this time I am serious. I have never understood why Justin agreed to maintain him in London. Richard is nearly thirty, and it is time we made some changes. It would be different if he were married, or if we were going up for the seasons, but we rarely go to Town."

Justina spoke in defense of her wayward brother. "I had such a lovely time during my season, Mamma. And Richard was an absolute darling about hosting me and escorting me to all the important balls and operas. I had a jolly time."

"That may be, but since then we have barely seen him. Or before, truth be told. You are head of the family now, Timothy, so do tell me if you disagree. But I cannot help thinking this long absence from his family, not to mention access to a seemingly bottomless purse, have not been good for Richard."

"I don't disagree. But let us enjoy Christmas before we worry about all that, hm?"

Her mother-in-law's face puckered. "I shall try. But without Richard here . . . Oh, I knew he would not come!"

"Wrong again, Mamma, for here I am."

Lady Barbara turned with an audible gasp. "Richard! My dear boy. I knew you would come!"

Rachel saw her brother-in-law's eyebrows rise doubtfully at her words.

Lady Barbara waved dismissively. "Oh, you know I always think the worst, to protect myself from disappointment. But here you are!"

She held out both hands to him. He took them and dutifully kissed her cheek.

Rachel did not know Timothy's brother well, although they had met several times over the years. He was handsome, charming, and a few years younger than Timothy. Both men were tall with high cheekbones and dark hair, but Richard's eyes were blue, whereas Timothy's were brown.

A small dog came tap-tapping into the room. A fluffy tan-and-ginger terrier wearing a waistcoat and cravat.

Lady Barbara frowned at it. "Who let this creature inside?"

"He's mine, Mamma," Richard replied. "I assumed you wouldn't mind."

"He had better be house-trained and not harass my pug." She gestured toward the plump dog asleep on the sofa. As if in reply, the pug gave an obligatory growl before closing its eyes once more.

"He shall be a perfect gentleman, unlike me," Richard said, then glanced around. "I did ask Pickering to hold on to him until I could greet you properly, but—"

A man stuck his silvery head into the doorway, expression mildly offended. "I should like to see you hold on to that cur when he's bent on wriggling from your grasp."

Lady Barbara seemed nearly as surprised to see the older man as she had the dog. "Pickering? Are you still alive?"

"Appearance to the contrary, yes, my lady."

"Good heavens, you look old."

"A pleasure to see you too"—he added a little jab—"dowager." Then the gruff valet continued up the stairs with case and valises.

A second man stood waiting awkwardly just outside the doorway, hat in hand. Lady Barbara looked from him to Richard, brows high in question.

Noticing, Richard said, "Pray forgive me! Come in, Murray, come in. Mamma, allow me to introduce my friend, Mr. David Murray. Murray, this is my mother, Lady Barbara."

"How do you do."

Richard continued the introductions. "My brother, Sir Timothy, and his wife, Lady Brockwell."

"Rachel," she interjected with a smile.

"And you remember my sister, Justina."

Justina curtsied. "We met in London, yes. Good to see you again, Mr. Murray."

"And you, Miss Brockwell."

Richard addressed his mother. "I have invited Mr. Murray to spend Christmas with us. I knew you would not mind another guest."

His mother hesitated. "Oh. I . . ."

The other man said earnestly, "I hope it is not too much of an imposition. Richard was most persuasive in his invitation."

Richard clapped his shoulder. "Murray here has no family to spend Christmas with. I knew you would want to make him welcome."

"I . . . see. Then by all means. We shall make up the numbers, somehow."

Rachel added more warmly, "You are very welcome, Mr. Murray."

Richard looked at the long-case clock and grimaced. "Sorry to be late. Our coach was delayed. A boy fell from the roof, and the coachman felt it necessary to stop for him."

"I should hope so!" Justina said on an indignant laugh. "Is he all right?"

"Remarkably unscathed. Though he has a lump the size of a cricket ball."

His mother asked, "No one we know, I hope?"

"Does that make it less concerning? No—an apprentice bound for Wishford."

The butler, Carville, entered to announce, "Dinner is served."

"Shall we go and change, Mamma?" asked Richard. "Or will you put up with us as we are?"

Again she hesitated. "We don't want the meal to be spoilt, so we will make an exception about dressing for dinner this once, especially as our houseguests don't arrive until tomorrow. Let Carville take your coats and hats, and perhaps Mr. Murray might like to . . . freshen up a bit?"

Richard looked at his friend and noticed his untidy hair and chapped face.

"Mr. Murray was goodness itself and gave his inside seat to the fallen apprentice," he explained.

"That was well done, Mr. Murray," Timothy said with a nod of approval.

Richard shepherded his friend toward the door. "Just give us five minutes."

When the men left them, Rachel's mother-in-law sighed. "Leave it to Richard to bring home not one stray but two."

"Mamma," Justina mildly objected. "Mr. Murray is very amiable and a successful publisher. And the dog is adorable."

"Well, we will make the best of it." Lady Barbara pointed emphatically toward the door. "But if he bothers my pug, out he goes."

Justina's dimples appeared. "The stray dog or the stray man?"

"Either one!"

A short while later, Richard and his friend rejoined the others and sat down to dinner.

His sister-in-law smiled at their guest and said, "Mr. Murray, do tell us something about yourself."

The man shrugged modestly. "I wish there were more to tell. I operate a small printing and publishing company in London. Just like a hundred other hopefuls."

"Do you publish books?" Rachel asked, an appreciative gleam in her eyes. As the proprietor of Ivy Hill's circulating library, his sister-in-law had a special interest in books.

"No. A magazine and other small publications."

"I see. Well, those are important too."

Lady Barbara looked from Murray to Richard. "And how do you two know each other?"

Murray began, "Richard here is one of my—"

Richard nudged his foot under the table. He had asked Murray not to mention his writing. The articles he wrote were published anonymously.

". . . friends," Murray blurted. "And a great reader."

"And Mr. Murray is all modesty," Richard added. "His magazine is very popular in London."

"Among a certain set, yes, though I could wish for more subscribers . . . and profits."

His mother smiled coolly. "Perhaps we ought to leave discussions of business until after the ladies withdraw."

"I don't mind," Rachel said. "I find publishing most interesting."

"My wife started our town's circulating library," Sir Timothy explained.

"Commendable. I salute you, Lady Brockwell."

"Thank you. I had a great deal of help in getting started. I still review the accounts and subscriber lists regularly, and give the manager a few hours leisure each week, but I am not as involved in the day-to-day as I used to be before our child was born."

Richard felt David's surprised gaze on his profile. Had he failed to mention the addition to the family? Apparently.

He cleared his throat. "That reminds me. How is . . . my little nephew?" Richard squirmed. What had they named him? His mother had written with the news, but it had been months ago.

His mother replied, "My grandson is in excellent health."

Would no one remind him of the boy's name?

Rachel smiled, apparently taking pity on him. "Frederick will soon be asleep if Nurse Pocket has her way, but I will introduce him to you tomorrow."

Frederick. That was it. At least they had not named the child Justin, after their father. Richard smiled back. "I shall look forward to making his acquaintance."

The meal progressed. While they were eating dessert, Justina asked, "Are you still writing, Richard? When I stayed with you in London, I remember you scratching away at something every morning. A novel, was it?"

Richard shrugged, feeling uncomfortably warm. "My laundry list, no doubt." He preferred to keep his writing secret until if and when his book was published.

His mother looked doubtful. "A novel? Really, Justina. Your brother has long been a gentleman of leisure, spending his time as he wishes."

"Very true, Mamma," Richard said. "Until now."

Sir Timothy turned to their guest, perhaps hoping to divert the conversation and its undercurrent of familial tension. "What is the name of your publication? Perhaps I have heard of it."

Murray told him.

"Ah. Political satire, is it not?"

"In part, yes. As well as other articles of interest to gentlemen."

"Gentlemen who share your political persuasion?"

"Well, yes. Though we do try to be fair and objective."

"Fair and objective?" Richard snorted. "Sorry, did I say that aloud?"

Lady Barbara rose. "And when the topic of politics is raised, then it is definitely time for the ladies to withdraw. Forgive me, Rachel, I know it is your place now, but I must insist."

"Very well." Rachel rose too, and Justina followed suit.

When the women departed, the three men talked for a while longer. Then Richard tried to interest his brother in a game of cards, but Sir Timothy begged off, saying he had an early morning. "The house party begins tomorrow."

Already? Richard inwardly groaned.

After his brother had left them to bid the ladies good night, Murray said wistfully, "If I had a wife as beautiful as Lady Brockwell, I wouldn't spend the evening with the pair of us either."

Richard said nothing. He'd spent a great deal of energy making sure he did not end up with a wife.

He and Murray lingered for a time over port and pipes, discussing parliament, news, and upcoming article ideas.

Eventually his friend claimed fatigue and retired to the guest room assigned to him.

Richard went to join the others in the drawing room but found only Justina within. They sat down to a game of draughts.

"What have I missed?" he asked. "Mamma wrote and told me you threw over Sir Cyril. That was well done."

"I am glad you approve. My friend Miss Bingley married him instead. Did Mamma also tell you I admire someone else?"

"No."

"Not surprising. She doesn't think he's good enough for me, which is silly. I think he's wonderful, and I hope you shall agree. In fact, I have been longing to introduce him to you."

"If it's Horace Bingley, I already know him as well as I need to."

"No, not Horace. He is a relative newcomer to Ivy Hill. Nicholas Ashford."

"Ashford?"

"Yes, a distant relation of Rachel's. He inherited Thornvale after her father died."

"Ah yes, I remember hearing about that. What does Mamma object to?"

She shrugged. "No title. New money. Worked for a living . . ."

Richard smirked. "Yes, drat those men with professions. How tedious. They make us men of leisure look bad."

Her dark eyes danced with humor. "Oh, Richard."

"Is Mr. Ashford to be one of the house party?"

"Yes. Thankfully Rachel wrote up the guest list rather than Mamma."

"Good, then I shall look forward to meeting him. Though, I will find it hard to think any man is good enough for you, Justi."

He reached across the games table and tweaked her chin.

She grinned. "And what about you, Richard? When are you going to meet someone and fall in love?"

"I do both regularly, I assure you. But if you are talking about marriage, I have no plans to fall into that trap."

She tilted her head to one side. "Why do you call it a trap?"

"Well, we didn't have the best example where happy marriage is concerned."

She blinked wide eyes. "Did we not?"

His little sister looked sincerely perplexed. She had been so young. Too young to understand.

"Never mind. I am just a confirmed old bachelor—that's all."

"I don't believe that for a moment. You just haven't met the right woman yet. Perhaps you will fall in love during the house party. Wouldn't that be a grand surprise?"

"A surprise indeed, especially as I believe I am already acquainted with everyone on the guest list."

"True. And our numbers are even smaller than expected. Sir Cyril and his bride were supposed to join us after their wedding trip, but we've received word their ship has been delayed."

"Lucky escape for us."

She ignored that. "However, his sisters will both be here— Penelope and Arabella Awdry. Both excellent women and unattached, though I believe Horace admires Penelope."

"Talk about grand surprises . . ." Richard murmured.

Justina went on, "Their mother, the dowager Lady Awdry, will join us because she would otherwise be alone at Christmas. Horace

Bingley will be here, but his parents are entertaining relatives, so they will stay home, though we are all invited to their house on New Year's Eve."

"I see. Then I think it is safe to say that the only romance in the offing this Christmas will be between Horace and Penelope and you and Mr. Ashford."

Her dimples blazed. "Oh, I hope there will be romance. I hope so indeed!"

Lady Barbara walked in and stopped near the games table, her speculative gaze moving from one to the other of her offspring.

"I overheard you two talking. I also hope for romance during the house party. Not for Justina, perhaps, but for you, Richard."

Richard grimaced, thinking, *Oh no, here we go. . . .*

He tried to divert her. "Yet Justina tells me she is quite taken with one of the young men coming to the house party. There is no need to waste time on me, when she is already inclined toward matrimony."

His mother replied, "Justina is young and will have other opportunities to meet an eligible gentleman. I had hoped Edward Winspear would accept our invitation, but alas, he sent his regrets. He is spending the holiday in Town this year."

"Lucky man," Richard quipped.

Her lips curved in a sour smile. "Justina is not yet twenty, but you are nearly thirty, Richard. It is time you married."

Richard's face stiffened. "I am aware of my age, Mamma."

"There is one woman in particular I wish you to spend time with during the house party. Arabella Awdry."

"I have met the Miss Awdrys in the past, Mamma."

"You may have met Arabella in passing, but it has been several years since you have spent any time in each other's company."

"I remember her as a skinny, silly, giggling thing, forever making doe eyes at me."

"I think you will find her much improved."

"If she is so wonderful, why didn't Timothy marry her? I recall that once being your aim."

"You know why. His heart has long been attached elsewhere. But Arabella is lovely and accomplished and would make an excellent wife."

"Mamma . . ." Justina tsked. "You have just crushed any hope of Richard pursuing Arabella. You must realize that if you push him in her direction, he will do the opposite, just to spite you."

Richard nodded his agreement. His sister knew him too well.

"I sincerely hope that is not the case."

After his mother retired, Richard talked to Justina for half an hour longer, then finally trudged up to his old room, kept for him all these years, though he rarely visited.

There were his old books and memorabilia of his school days and his time at university—good memories and bad. In the wardrobe hung a few out-of-fashion frockcoats and pantaloons, worn gloves, riding boots, and a perfectly good beaver hat he'd forgotten about. Ah well, he'd bought himself others.

He saw the hinged wooden box on his bookcase—a beautiful box of polished acacia wood. Seth, his boyhood friend, had brought it home on his first leave.

He would never have allowed himself otherwise, but he was feeling unusually nostalgic. He opened the box and peered inside. Empty, except for the single letter Seth had sent him before he died. But it wasn't really Seth he was thinking of. It was Seth's sister, Susanna, whose face flickered through his mind. And with her memory, came the guilt.

He slammed the lid shut.

CHAPTER

Three

True to Justina's prediction, Richard decided to make sure his first encounter with Arabella Awdry went poorly indeed. He planned to make it abundantly clear from the outset that he had no interest in her, or in marriage in general.

That way she would not weary herself or him throughout the rest of the holiday by mooning after him, and she could cast her hook at someone else instead. And then Mamma, seeing it was hopeless, would let off the pressure as well. Yes, he would have to shoulder his mother's cold anger, but he was used to her disapproval, and better that than a simpering female following him around like a lost puppy throughout the twelve days of Christmas. One besotted pet was enough.

He spent the day working on revisions and then enjoyed an hour respite, during which he easily bested Murray in two games of billiards.

In the evening, he dressed with care, tying his cravat into a fussy waterfall style Pickering would never have managed. He then directed his valet to shave points into his side-whiskers and curl and arrange his hair over his brow in Brutus style.

"Curl, sir?"

"Yes, curl."

Pickering's frown betrayed his opinion, but he said in his weary monotone, "Very good, sir."

When he was finished, Richard asked, "Well, how do I look?"

"Like a fop, sir."

Richard beamed. "Excellent."

He left his room at last. Wally, similarly attired, trotted beside him.

He met David Murray at the top of the stairs, and his friend glanced at him once, and then again, but made no comment. Murray looked uncomfortable in one of Richard's evening coats, which fit him a bit snugly. Thankfully, Pickering had tacked up the too-long sleeves.

As they descended together, Murray whispered, "I am out of my depth here, man. Sure to call a duke a sir or a sir a lord. Lord help me."

Richard grinned. "No dukes or lords to worry about tonight."

"Thank heaven for that."

The houseguests began to arrive. Richard led Murray into the billiards room and from its threshold quietly appraised the players assembling in the hall.

The first was a young man of average height with light brown hair, fair eyes, and a ready smile. "That's Horace Bingley. Good-hearted fellow, bruising rider, though a bit of a dunderhead."

"How do I address him?"

"'Mr. Bingley, I hear you are an excellent rider.' You shan't edge in a word after that."

He pointed next to a woman who matched Horace's height and nearly his breadth of shoulder, with plain features and thin brown hair. "That big-boned Amazon is Sir Cyril Awdry's sister Penelope. She's twice the man her bird-witted brother is."

Murray swallowed. "And I call her . . . ?"

"Whenever you need a second in a fight or want to be bested in a shooting competition."

His mother's pug trotted across the hall and sat at Penelope's feet. Wally, not to be outdone, went over to join them. Richard hoped the dogs did not mistake the tall woman for a tree.

Richard's gaze swept the hall. "They have a younger sister too. But I don't see her at the moment."

From behind them, soft footprints approached. A lithe figure swept past and into the hall. Murray started, and Richard felt a pinch of unease. He had not realized anyone was there. One of the female guests visiting the indoor water closet at the end of the passage, perhaps. How much had she overheard?

The willowy female approached his mother, engaging her in low conversation, her back to them, her posture excellent. Her honey blond hair was styled in a simple coiffure, and she wore a fashionable ivory gown with a lower waistline that accentuated her trim, delicately curved torso.

Richard took a deep breath. "Well, we had better join the others before Mamma sends out a search party."

As they slipped into the hall, his mother caught sight of him. "Ah, here is Richard now."

The female turned. He catalogued a proud bearing, fine features, slender neck, and exquisite collarbones.

His mother said, "You remember Miss Arabella Awdry?"

Richard cast the young woman a purposely blank look, then turned to his parent. "I . . . believe so." Richard did remember Arabella Awdry, but he didn't want to encourage her or his mother. So he'd delivered his opening gambit as he'd intended, but he'd almost faltered. Arabella was far prettier than he recalled.

"Don't be foolish, Richard. Of course you do. You two have met on several occasions in the past."

"The distant past, Lady Barbara," Miss Awdry said evenly. "No doubt Mr. Brockwell meets many, *many* women in his whirlwind social life."

"True." He fluffed his cravat and flashed a disarming smile at her sister. "Now you, Miss Penelope, I do recall. You make a big impression wherever you go."

Arabella shot him a look.

He innocently met her gaze. "What? I meant it as a compliment."

Horace Bingley laughed somewhat nervously. "I quite agree, Brockwell. Miss Awdry is unforgettable."

Lady Barbara ended the awkward moment by turning to introduce Lady Lillian, Penelope and Arabella's mother.

Richard then introduced his friend Murray to the others in the party.

Nicholas Ashford arrived, and Justina led him forward to introduce him to Richard, hope and worry sparking in her eyes. That she should desire *his* approval was touching and rather humbling. He did not deserve such regard.

"Richard, I would like you to meet Mr. Ashford. Mr. Ashford, my brother, Richard Brockwell."

"How do you do."

The young man gave an awkward bow, his smooth boyish face ill at ease. Mr. Ashford was above average height and thin, making him appear perhaps taller than he was. He had light brown hair and bluish-green eyes. *Not good enough for Justina* was his instant judgment. But then he surveyed the man's fine striped waistcoat, pristine cravat, and expertly tailored coat and altered his opinion.

Rachel joined them. "Oh good. I see you two gentlemen have met." She added, "Nicholas is my distant cousin and the master of Thornvale."

Richard nodded. "So Justina has told me."

Nicholas Ashford reddened and said diffidently, "'Master' sounds so grand. I am just a man, trying to do my duty by Thornvale."

"And I am sure you do so admirably," Justina soothed.

The young man's shy, admiring gaze rested on his little sister. Looking from one to the other, Richard felt an odd parental pain in his chest as he realized he was no longer first in Justina's heart.

At the appointed time, they all sat down to dinner. At Richard's command, Wally sat outside the dining room door and watched the meal from a respectable distance, though the dog clearly longed to partake. Richard glanced at him, for a moment wishing he could be outside the room as well. His mother had arranged for him to sit next to Arabella. Thankfully, Lady Lillian had maneuvered Horace directly across from her and next to Penelope. Chatty Mr. Bingley talked eagerly to both sisters, leaving Richard in relative peace.

Soon Arabella turned to Mr. Murray and engaged him in intelligent conversation, asking about his background, his magazine, and the world of publishing.

Richard began to feel a little left out.

Idiot, he chastised himself. Was this not what he wanted? To discourage any attachments? *Stick with the plan, Brockwell.*

After the women withdrew and the men were alone in the dining room, Murray leaned near him and hissed, "Are you insane? Miss Awdry is an angel. An absolute angel. And if you can't see that, then you are the dunderhead, not Mr. Bingley."

Richard shrugged. "If you are so smitten, perhaps you ought to pursue her yourself."

"As if she would ever seriously consider a man like me."

It was likely true, Richard silently assented, but to his friend, he said, "You never know. Silly females sometimes surprise one."

Eventually, they joined the women in the drawing room.

As soon as he entered, Justina took him aside. "What do you think of Mr. Ashford?"

"He seems an agreeable—if somewhat shy—young man. Do you truly like him?"

Eyes shining, Justina nodded. "I do."

"Then I shall like him too."

She squeezed him arm. "I knew you would."

They all conversed for a time, but soon Justina begged for dancing. A troubled frown crossed Rachel's face. "I have engaged someone to play for us later in the week but had not thought we would dance tonight. . . ."

The dowager Lady Awdry rose stiffly. "I shall play, if no one objects. That way, all the young ladies can dance. I am not familiar with the latest pieces but can play a French cotillion and several English country dances."

Justina smiled at her. "Thank you, Lady Lillian." She turned expectant eyes on Richard. He was surprised she would wish to dance with him with Mr. Ashford in attendance but would not miss his chance to dance with his little sister. Who knew how many more he would have?

He danced the first set with Justina while Horace danced with Arabella, Mr. Ashford with Penelope, and Rachel with Timothy. Murray sat out, looking ill-at-ease near Lady Barbara. Richard danced the second with Rachel, the other guests changing partners among themselves. He saw Lady Lillian tiring and began to think he would manage to avoid dancing with Arabella that night.

"One more!" Justina pleaded.

Lady Lillian replied, "Very well, but only one. I am done in."

He decided to ask his mother for the last, and when he turned, there she stood. Wearing a grim, determined smile, she took Arabella's arm and led her toward Richard in a rare lapse of tact.

"Richard, you have not yet danced with Miss Awdry. An oversight, I'm sure."

Mortification flushed Miss Awdry's cheeks. She looked down a moment, then rallied, raising her chin. "Indeed, my lady, I have not the least intention of dancing another. My slippers pinch."

"Come, Miss Awdry, it is clear you take great pleasure in dancing."

"The pleasure depends on the partner," Arabella murmured.

Even Richard could not refuse in the face of his mother's bold attack. Miss Awdry looked embarrassed enough already. And so dashed pretty . . .

He bowed. "I have been remiss indeed. May I have the next, Miss Arabella?"

"I . . ." She looked ready to refuse but faltered. "Thank you."

Richard noticed the two matriarchs share conspiratorial looks of triumph.

When his mother moved away, Arabella quietly hissed, "Please don't assume I asked your mother to do that."

"I don't. I saw the maternal force sweeping you along in her wake."

She nodded. "Neither of our mothers is very subtle, I agree."

The dance began.

As they bowed to one another and changed places, she said, "I suppose you dance a great deal in London?"

"No."

"But you must be invited to many grand balls."

"True."

They stepped through another pattern in silence, then she huffed. "I don't care a fig either way, but politeness dictates we should have some conversation."

"Does it?"

"Are we to have silence the entire set? I don't remember you ever being at a loss for words before."

Another turn, and then they were standing out for a round at the bottom of the line. She tried again. "Were I one of your London debutantes, what would you talk about?"

He made no answer.

She said coolly, "I realize you are doing your utmost not to show me any marked attention, but by treating me with cold disdain rather than with the politeness you showed your other partners, you are singling me out indeed."

He looked at her a moment, then tried a different tactic. "If you were a debutante, I would not be dancing with you, let alone talking to you. Now, if you were a wealthy widow . . ." He waggled his eyebrows and let the comment dangle.

She stared at him, mouth ajar. Speechless.

He took her hand again, preparing to rejoin the dance, but she withdrew her fingers from his grasp.

"Excuse me. I feel the need to go wash my hands." She turned away in disgust.

Richard felt momentary triumph, but it quickly faded.

Murray appeared at his elbow. "Well done. You were dancing with the handsomest woman in the room."

Richard shrugged. "Not my type."

"No? What type is she?"

"Marriageable."

Richard slipped out the door, retreating into that male bastion, the billiards room.

The *tap tap tap* of heeled slippers came down the passage a few minutes later—Miss Awdry on her way back from the water closet, no doubt. He was surprised when she entered the room.

He turned, a lazy smirk on his lips, and saw that her eyes were blazing mad.

Arabella marched toward him like an advancing soldier. "Now that I've had a moment to think, let me make something abundantly clear." She drew herself up, her face flushed a delicate pink. "I have no interest in you, Richard Brockwell. I know you enjoy shocking people, but I am already familiar with your libertine reputation and would not accept you under any circumstances. So you can stop being rude, and we can both go back to pretending to enjoy the party for our families' sakes. It is Christmastime, after all. And while I have your attention, I warn you not to say another word against my sister. She is *not* 'twice the man her brother is.' She is a woman, with a woman's heart and feelings. Not that you've ever cared about a woman's feelings, except perhaps Justina's. I will not tolerate any criticism of my beloved sister, any more than you would tolerate criticism of yours."

"But mine is younger and doesn't outweigh me by three stones."

She slapped his face. Hard.

He schooled his expression, determined not to wince. Instead, he coolly turned his face and offered her the other cheek.

Her small nostrils flared.

"And my brother may not possess the sharp wit that you so heartlessly wield to injure others, but he is a kind, decent, and respectable man who does not deserve your cutting sarcasm. He is a far better man than you will ever be."

Richard sobered. "You are absolutely right."

For a moment she stilled, as if sifting his reply for latent insult, but finding none, she turned and stalked across the room.

At the door, she turned back. "If I hear any more unkind comments about my family, you will leave me no choice but to say something unkind about you, something I have kept secret for a decade. Don't try me."

She whirled away and quit the room.

Richard's head pounded. Arabella might be genteel and ladylike in most respects, but clearly slights to her family brought out the worst in her. Or was it the best? Watching her regal posture as she strode away, head held high, Richard felt reluctant admiration for the favored young woman.

Murray came in and stood beside him. "Sorry. I overheard some of that. What secret was she talking about?"

Richard feigned a dismissive air. "Who knows with women?"

Then he turned away and downed a glass of brandy. The truth was, Richard had more than one skeleton in his closet. Had she somehow learned of the secret he had promised never to tell? If so, he hoped she would keep it to herself forever.

Arabella Awdry marshaled all of her self-possession and returned to the drawing room. She pinned a benign smile to her face as she entered, not wanting anyone to guess the emotions churning in her stomach.

Richard Brockwell could try the patience of a saint, and she was no saint.

It was clear what he was doing. Their mothers were obviously trying to foster a courtship between them. Both women were marriage-minded, unlike Arabella herself. And Richard had clearly resolved not to fall in with their matchmaking schemes. Even so, he'd injured her pride. She reminded herself that she was considered pretty, accomplished, and from an upstanding old family, even if her brother was something of a rattle. A lovable rattle, in her point of view.

And Penelope was the best sister a girl could have—a dear, loyal sister. Even though Pen was a few years older and certainly taller, she was also more vulnerable. Aware of how she stood out, self-conscious of her size and less-obvious femininity. Arabella had felt protective of her ever since the neighborhood boys began teasing her as an adolescent. Insults—veiled and not—seemed to roll off their brother, Cyril, like water from a duck, but Penelope took them to heart.

It was not the first time Arabella had slapped Richard Brockwell. As youths at a family party years ago, Richard had called Penelope a "horse godmother," slang for a large, masculine woman. And Arabella had stalked up to him and slapped his face. Hard.

The man would never change. If anything, he had grown worse.

Arabella had not wanted to come to this house party, but her mother had eagerly accepted the invitation for them when she learned Horace Bingley, Nicholas Ashford, and Richard Brockwell—three most eligible gentlemen—had also been invited.

Penelope had also seemed conflicted about the invitation and wondered aloud if they could not simply stay home at Broadmere and enjoy a quiet Christmas together.

Arabella understood her sister's reluctance. Horace Bingley had once expressed interest in Penelope, but more than a year had passed, and he had not acted upon that interest.

Their mother had argued, "But my dears, Lady Barbara has assured me that Richard will be coming to Brockwell Court for Christmas this year. We don't want to miss an opportunity to renew our acquaintance with him."

Do we not? Arabella had thought cynically. But aloud she'd said, "Lady Barbara always says that, and he never comes."

That's right, Arabella had reminded herself. Richard would probably not be there, so why not go? Justina was great fun, and Sir Timothy and his wife, Rachel, were charming. And the dowager Lady Brockwell was always kind to her too, though she knew others found her intimidating.

Penelope had said, "Mamma, Cyril may not be comfortable spending time at Brockwell Court."

"Comfortable? Why should he not be comfortable?" Now that Cyril had married, their mother seemed ready to forget that Justina jilted him. She flipped her wrist. "Oh, he may have briefly considered an alliance with Miss Brockwell, but that is all in the past. He and his wife are due home a few days before the party begins. I am sure they will wish to join us."

Cyril would want to go, Arabella had guessed. Perhaps in part to show off his blissful wedded state, when Justina was not yet betrothed. No, that wasn't likely. Her brother was not spiteful in the least.

Penelope had twisted her long fingers. "I can see what you are thinking, Mamma. But forcing Horace and me into each other's company will only be awkward for everyone. I doubt he will act now, if he hasn't already."

"Well, it will be a good opportunity for both of you girls. You should keep your options open. At Brockwell Court, you will spend time with Horace, Richard, and Nicholas Ashford as well."

Arabella shook her head. "Mamma. Mr. Ashford is clearly in love with Justina Brockwell."

"Perhaps, but they are not yet engaged."

"Only because her mother has asked them to wait until Justina comes of age. And Justina wants him to become acquainted with *dear Richard* first, and the selfish man can't be bothered to come home."

Then their mother had sweetened the bargain by mentioning something sure to sway Penelope to her side. "And Sir Timothy will no doubt take you and Cyril shooting."

"Shooting?" Penelope perked up at the word. "I would enjoy that, of course. And I would like to visit Locke stables while we're in Ivy Hill. Cyril and I have our sights set on a pair of matched hunters."

Their mother beamed. "There, you see? It's perfect. Something or someone for everyone." Here, she had sent Arabella a knowing smile.

In the end, Arabella acquiesced. Her mother and sister wished to go, and she would not suspend their happiness for the world. Especially at Christmas.

She had consoled herself by recalling that Brockwell Court was located in the village of Ivy Hill, whereas Broadmere was a rural country estate. She remembered Justina talking with fondness about Christmases in Ivy Hill, with caroling and church bells, fetes and dancing. And best of all, the Brockwells were always charitable at Christmastime. When she'd pressed for details, Justina had described preparing baskets of food for village widows and other poor families, visits to the almshouse, and gifts given to the servants on Boxing Day. Perhaps she could also participate in those activities while they stayed at Brockwell Court. That notion appealed to her very much indeed.

In her heart of hearts, what Arabella really wanted was to live in London with Aunt Genevieve and join her charity work. Her mother, however, would not countenance the idea. Aunt Gen's bluestocking, campaigning ways were all right for a spinster of a certain age, but not for her beautiful, accomplished younger daughter. Her mother had set her hopes on Arabella marrying soon and marrying well. She and Papa had been so happy together, and she wanted that for her children too, she argued. Was it not only natural that she should?

But Arabella was determined not to be pressured into marriage. Only the truest love would convince her to wed. And she would certainly never marry a man who would not remain faithful to her, a man she could not trust.

Thanks to a modest inheritance coming to her, she did not need a husband to support her. She was blessed with the freedom to choose to marry or not, a luxury denied to many women. And she planned to make the most of that blessing. She longed to make her life count, to make a difference.

In the meantime, Christmas at Brockwell Court might give her an opportunity to serve her fellow man and enjoy a small taste of Aunt Gen's life.

She had thought, *Now if only Richard Brockwell does not come home and spoil things. . . .*

But he had.

No, Arabella decided anew. She would not let Richard Brockwell spoil her Christmas . . . or her plans.

CHAPTER

Four

In the morning, Richard awoke, his head pounding.

Not only was his head pounding, but someone outside was pounding as well. Could a man get no rest? So much for the quiet of the country!

With a groan, he rolled out of bed and slogged to the window, ready to beg mercy from whichever gardener was hammering stakes, or whichever kitchen maid was beating some poor chicken senseless. Folding back the shutters, what he saw sealed his lips.

In the orangey-grey light of a December morning, a group of elderly women marched up the drive, their leader beating a pot with a wooden spoon. Some wore black capes and others red cloaks. They descended upon Brockwell Court like a flock of crows and redbirds. These were the beldames of the parish, bent and withered, going from house to house, starting, apparently, with the great house. Richard glanced at the mantel clock with a sigh. Not yet eight.

A double rap sounded, and his door creaked open behind him. David Murray entered his room, hurriedly dressed except for coat and cravat, no doubt drawn by the hubbub.

"What is going on?" he whispered.

"Good morning. You're just in time to witness an old custom in rural England." Richard gestured toward the window.

Crossing the room, Murray looked out at the women. His brow furrowed. "Beggars?"

"Not on St. Thomas Day. On this day, it's considered their due. Poor widows go mumping. In some places it's called Thomasing or a-gooding. They collect small gifts of money or food to help them celebrate Christmas."

"Interesting . . ." David murmured.

Below, the front door opened, and Sir Timothy and Rachel stepped out.

The group leader said, "Here we come a mumpin'. Pray, remember St. Thomas Day and give us something toward the keepin' up o' Christmas."

Then she led out in a warbling treble voice, and all the women joined her in singing:

> "Little Cock Robin sat on a wall,
> We wish you a merry Christmas, and a great snowfall,
> Apples to eat and nuts to crack,
> We wish you a merry Christmas, with a rap, tap, tap."

Richard winced. Enough already with the rap, tap, tap!

Then a solemn procession began with each woman approaching the lord and lady of the manor. Sir Timothy produced a sixpence for each from a leather purse, while Rachel handed out small bags—likely filled with wheat and parcels of tea, both of which were very dear.

In return, the women gave their benefactors sprigs of mistletoe or holly they had gathered.

Rachel smiled and announced, "Thank you, ladies. Please do come around to the kitchen. Cook has some cake and a cup of hot coffee for each of you."

"That reminds me," Murray said at his elbow. "I'm starving. All right if I finish dressing and head down to the breakfast room, or shall I wait for you?"

"You go ahead."

Richard glanced down at the mumpers once more. A woman at the back of the group looked up. With her hooded cloak, he'd not seen her face earlier, but now he recognized her with a jolt. Mrs. Reeves. The mother of his boyhood friend, Seth, and his pretty sister, Susanna.

The past came rushing back. Oh, the many happy hours Richard had spent in their cottage as a lad. Honeycroft had been a place of warmth, acceptance, and good-natured teasing, a welcome refuge after the chilly propriety and expectations of Brockwell Court. Richard had enjoyed sharing meals with the Reeves family, joining in with their jokes and laughter. At least until Seth had enlisted and Richard had spoiled things with Susanna.

But there was no laughter in Mrs. Reeves's face today. How the years had aged her. Richard knew Seth had died during the war, as so many had, and he'd heard Susanna had married one of his shipmates and gone to live on the coast somewhere. Richard had not given their mother much thought in recent years, but how shocking to see her now, among Ivy Hill's poor widows. Her husband had died a few years before, but he'd assumed Mrs. Reeves had gone stoically on, managing fairly well on her own.

Regret washed over him, and then a foreign feeling rose in his chest—the desire to help her. He turned away from the window, trying to stifle the urge by focusing his mind on the important question of which coat to wear instead.

Wally looked up at him from the little cushion bed Richard had packed in his trunk.

"What do you think, Walt? The green? The blue? The dark blue?"

Wally barked.

"Dark blue it is."

Later that morning, after Rachel bid the last of her elderly visitors farewell, she prepared for the next project on her list. Miss Arabella, Justina, and Lady Barbara joined her in the servants' hall to assemble the baskets they would soon deliver to the residents of Ivy Hill's almshouse and to other housebound villagers.

Willow baskets, from Belle Island in Berkshire, were spread out on the large table. Together the women began layering in the contents: a small lap rug, two handkerchiefs, and a pair of warm, knitted gloves for each, all made by volunteers of the Ladies Tea and Knitting Society over the last few months with material donated by the local dressmaker.

There were also a few candles purchased from Mrs. O'Brien, the local chandler. And finally, parcels of tea, a mincemeat pie, a wedge of Barton cheese, and a small jar of jam made in the Brockwell Court kitchen. A fresh quartern loaf from Craddock's bakery would be added just before delivery.

The women moved around the table, laying in the offerings one by one, chatting companionably as they did so.

Arabella asked if she might tie ribbon bows on each to add a festive touch. The idea was met with eager approval. Rachel happily collected the appropriate ribbon from the sewing room, and the baskets were soon festooned.

Richard poked his head inside. "Ah. Wondered what was going on in here. Sounded like a henhouse or a political rally."

He grinned and turned to go, but Justina called him back.

"Don't wander off, Richard. We are going to gather in the drawing room to practice caroling later."

"Caroling? Egad. Not I."

"Why not?"

"Someone must stay home to receive other carolers. It wouldn't do for the great house to be empty when the singing zealots come 'round."

Every year, the manor received carolers who came singing "Here We Come A-wassailing," "I Saw Three Ships Come Sailing In," and "We Wish You a Merry Christmas." They were rewarded with warm drinks or food—the requisite wassail or figgy pudding from Mrs. Nettleton's kitchen. But this year, Rachel had decided the Brockwell family and their guests would sing carols as well, in their home and at the almshouse.

Rachel felt her brow knit in mild concern. "I wonder if we have enough sheet music, considering all our guests. Perhaps I should send someone to the printer in Wishford."

"I'll go," Richard said. "That will be my contribution to the outing."

Rachel was surprised at his offer, and it seemed clear the others were too.

"Very well, Richard. Thank you." Rachel wrote down the hymns and song titles she wanted, adding, "We prefer the stationers in Salisbury—the printer there is far more pleasant—but Wishford is closer."

He glanced at the list. "And if he hasn't these, I assume I should pick up whatever sailor ditties he has in stock?"

Justina laughed. "Oh, Richard. You have such a ridiculous sense of humor! Don't worry, ladies, my brother is only teasing us."

"I certainly hope so," Rachel murmured, feeling far less convinced.

Eager for a respite from his mother and her houseguests, Richard eagerly prepared to set out on his errand. At the last minute, he decided he ought to invite Murray, thinking his friend might like to accompany him. But when he stopped at his room, he found Murray softly snoring atop atop his made bed with a book of verse tented over his chest. Richard decided to let him sleep.

He put on a greatcoat over his dark blue wool and donned a beaver hat. He wrapped a warm muffler around his neck, and a miniature one around Wally's neck, the dog as eager to be out of the house as he was. Then Richard went to the stables and asked a groom to harness up the curricle. They did not keep horses or carriage in London, which was a pity. Therefore, he had not driven in some time. Richard hoped he could still handle the ribbons with skill. In his younger days, he'd been known as quite a whip, and hopefully the old touch would return to him.

In his brother's curricle, Richard and Wally drove down the hill and followed the road into Wishford. The wind bit Richard's cheeks. Still, the fresh air and quiet were a relief. Wally seemed to relish the ride as well, paws on the front panel, wind blowing the hair from his eyes, tongue lolling happily.

The day was cold and crisp, the sky frosty blue. Richard could see his own breath, and the horses' besides. The trip was only a few miles, and with relief he soon reached Wishford, already thinking of stopping at the Crown to warm up before heading back.

He drove to the livery and left the horse and curricle in the care of a groom, then he and Wally strode around the churchyard and down the street until he came to the print shop. The sign read:

FRANCIS KNOCK
LETTERPRESS PRINTER
MUSIC SELLER & STATIONER
FARMERS' ACCOUNT BOOKS & LEDGERS

Richard looked through the window and saw Jamie Fleming, the young apprentice they'd met on the journey from London. He was returning metal type slugs to their appropriate slots in the drawers, his tongue tip protruding in concentration as he did so. Nearby, a broad-shouldered man stood at a wooden press, dabbing ink over the set type with sheepskin inking balls before positioning the paper and sliding the frame under the press, pulling the handle to make the impression.

Thin ropes like a laundress's clothesline crossed the interior, pages clipped to them and hanging to dry—broadsheets, advertisements, and more.

Seeing him through the glass, Jamie waved vigorously, accidentally knocking a few slugs to the floor. In a flash, the man stalked toward him, reeled back his hand, and—

Richard shoved open the door just as Jamie protectively covered his head. The door slammed against the wall with a bang, shaking the glass. Startled by the intrusion, the printer hesitated, then dropped his hand.

The big, brawny man had a belly gone to fat. He needed a shave, and it was only early afternoon. His hands were ink stained and curled as though habitually fisted.

Richard decided a civil approach might be best. Seeing Jamie's face redden in humiliation to be caught cowering, he thought an indirect approach might be merciful to the boy as well.

"Good day, my good fellows," Richard called out cheerfully. "Mr. Knock, I presume?"

"That's right."

"I hope I have not come at a bad time?"

"No, sir. Just training my clumsy apprentice here."

Richard looked at the boy as if just noticing him. "I say, is that you, Jamie? Jamie Fleming? What a pleasure to see you again, my boy."

"An-And you, sir."

Richard beamed at the printer. "I hope you realize what a treasure you have in young Fleming here, Mr. Knock." Richard noticed bruises on the boy's arms. From his fall from the coach, or had the printer inflicted them?

The man's eyes narrowed. "You are acquainted with this boy?"

"I am indeed. We are fast friends. But pray forgive me." Richard bowed. "Richard Brockwell of Brockwell Court. Heard of it?" He did not normally flaunt his connection to Ivy Hill's most prominent family but in this case thought it might be effective.

"'Course I have. Everyone knows Brockwell Court. What can I do for you, Mr. Brockwell?"

Richard handed over the list. "I came for sheet music. But now that I see Jamie is working here, I shall visit again. Often. To make sure all is well with him." He smiled at the lad but hoped the brute printer took his meaning—the lad might be an orphan, but he was not friendless. Might that knowledge be enough to curtail the man's abuse?

While the printer went to look for the requested sheet music, Richard winked at the boy.

Jamie dipped his head, grinning, but clearly hoping Mr. Knock would not see the expression. His gaze rested on Wally. "Your dog looks very dapper today, sir."

"Thank you, Jamie. Knew I liked you—you have excellent taste." With a glance at the printer, he lowered his voice, "I would ask how you are getting on here, but . . ."

"Oh, it's not so bad," Jamie hurried to reply. "There's a lot to learn, and I am slow and clumsy."

"I am sure that is not the case. Well, clumsy maybe, considering our first meeting, but not slow." He smiled. "You are clever, Jamie. I hope things improve here."

The boy smiled back. "Me too."

As he returned the curricle to the Brockwell Court stables a short while later, Richard saw Horace, Penelope, Nicholas, and his brother walking back from a shoot—dogs, beaters, and boys to pick up with game bags following behind. Richard waved to them and went into the house.

In the hall, he encountered Rachel coming down the stairs, little Frederick in arms, wearing a linen gown. "Ah, here is Uncle Richard."

Richard walked forward and dutifully praised the little boy, who in all truth was quite the most handsome child he had ever seen, with fair skin, dark curls, and blue eyes. He naturally looked like his brother, but Richard saw a bit of himself around the eyes, though Rachel had blue eyes too.

"He is very handsome, except for the drool," Richard said. "When he is older, I shall teach him to dress. This gown he's wearing is years out of fashion."

Frederick pulled his hand from his mouth and extended it toward Richard, reaching for his nose. Richard captured the little hand and kissed it. The boy grinned, exposing two pearly teeth. Encouraged by his success, Richard blew a loud burst of air against the boy's chubby arm, which brought on a bout of giggles.

"Clearly, I am a prodigy at this," Richard said. "He loves me already."

Giggles of the female variety then reached him.

He turned and was embarrassed to find Justina—and worse, Arabella—in the doorway to the drawing room, watching his foolish antics.

"Glad you find me so diverting, ladies," he said. Avoiding Arabella's gaze, he laid the music on the pianoforte and turned away, ears unaccountably warm.

Retrieving his walking stick, he and Wally set out together. He told himself he was just going to take a look at Honeycroft and get the lay of the land. Nothing to be nervous about—he didn't have to knock if he chose not to.

They left Brockwell Court via the back door and followed the footpath over Pudding Brook. Wally was in his glory, wiry body shaking with excitement. Every fallen leaf, every sheep, cow, and rustic scent a new delight to investigate. Richard had to urge him back onto the path more than once when the dog strained his hold on the leash.

Richard's feet followed the familiar route to Honeycroft as if of their own volition. How often he had come this way as a youth.

As he stepped from Steeple Lane onto the wooded path, he was surprised to find it overgrown with weeds and scattered with fallen branches. At the track's end stood the cottage—thatched roof, whitewashed walls, small windows, stone chimney. For a moment, he saw it as it had once been. Pristine white trim, well-kept thatch, freshly painted garden gate, flowers in every window box, the cheery smell of woodsmoke wafting from its stout chimney.

He was suddenly a boy again, tromping along the lane, determined to avoid the main road . . . and his father. That was how he first saw it. That lamplit window, like a stage lit by gaslight. The family of four sitting at the table, hands clasped, heads bowed. A moment later came a whirl of passing bowls and platters, the rumble of friendly conversation punctuated by smiles and occasional laughter. Standing there, viewing that domestic scene of love and happiness, he had felt as he often did, like an outsider, looking in.

Then the scene had changed. And by some stroke of undeserved favor he'd found himself at that table. Formal politeness quickly fell away, and the family's good-natured roasting soon extended to him. As weeks, then months passed, he joined them for meals, often bringing gifts of game, grain, or fruit. He'd helped Mr. Reeves with the beehives and chopped wood for Mrs. Reeves. He'd fished the brook with Seth and joined him in teasing Susanna.

The Reeveses had shared all they had with him generously: delicious food, unconditional acceptance, and affection. He had felt himself almost a member of the family. Until things changed. His fault. Regret swept over Richard again, and he tried to blink it away.

Abruptly, the old images faded and current reality intruded. The cottage and gate were in sore need of paint, the chimney cracked and crumbling, the thatch in need of attention, and the garden in winter's ruin. In truth, the whole house was a picture of long neglect.

The bee skeps next claimed his attention. What would Mr. Reeves say to see his precious hives now? Several hackles were listing to the side, and one skep was missing its cover altogether, exposing the wintering bees to dampness and likely death.

Thunder and turf. Honeycroft was in a sad state.

Taking a deep breath, he walked to the front door and made a fist, hesitated, then forced himself to knock. Mrs. Reeves had liked him, he reminded himself. Besides, Susanna was married and living elsewhere. And even if she had told her mother what had transpired between them, that had been a long time ago. All Richard wanted to do was to greet her and see if there was anything he could do to help. The worst Mrs. Reeves could do was rebuff him, and he would survive that. After all, it was the least he deserved.

He heard the scrape of a chair, and his heart beat hard with each approaching footstep. A moment later the door opened. He braced himself to face Mrs. Reeves, but the breath left him and his stomach dropped. Susanna herself stood there, a girl of four or five in arms. She stared at him. He stared back, awkwardness pulsing between them.

She looked the same and yet different. Same dark brown hair, although pulled back instead of loose around her shoulders, same gently flaring nose and full lips. Her face seemed more angular, her cheeks thinner, and her eyes had lost that innocent sparkle. Her jaw jutted forward obstinately, her expression one of steely wariness. Susanna used to smile often, but she had no smile for him now.

The little girl's eyes fixed on Wally with interest, but she did not smile either. Instead, she stuck her thumb in her mouth.

A boy of seven or eight appeared beside Susanna and took her hand, standing almost protectively beside her. "Who is it, Mamma?"

She made no answer.

Unable to meet her gaze any longer, Richard looked at the boy instead. His heart squeezed. He was the very spit of Seth. Richard bent lower. "You don't know me, but I know who you are. You look just like your uncle Seth."

"Do I? I don't remember him."

"I do. Nearly every day."

A tense silence followed, and then Susanna said coolly, "This is Mr. Brockwell. A . . . neighbor."

Richard amended, "I was a friend of your uncle's, when we were young."

The boy said, "He died in the war."

"Yes, I heard. I am sorry."

"My papa died t—"

"To what do we owe this visit?" Susanna brusquely interrupted.

Richard swallowed. Susanna was a widow too? "I . . . saw your mother this morning, at the house."

She lowered her head, a flush of embarrassment mottling her face. "I told her not to go. We are not so destitute. She would not have gone Thomasing for herself. But with Peter and Hannah here . . . well, she wants them to have a cheery Christmas."

"To be sure she does. That's why I came. To ask if she needs any—"

"We have all we need, thank you."

"Susanna? Who is it?" Mrs. Reeves called from somewhere behind her.

"It is Mr. Brockwell, Mamma."

The older woman appeared, wiping her hands on her apron. "Richard? Goodness me."

"Mrs. Reeves. A pleasure to see you. I have come home for Christmas and wanted to call to see how you were getting on. I did not realize Susanna would be home."

The younger woman said, "I am Mrs. Evans now."

Mrs. Reeves sent a concerned glance from one to the other. "My dear, we need not stand on formalities with old friends." She looked back at Richard. "Susanna and the children arrived a few weeks ago. Her husband died recently. Injured during the same war that took my Seth and never recovered."

"I am sorry."

The boy lowered himself to his haunches to study Wally skeptically. "Why is your dog dressed like you?"

For the first time in his brief span as a pet owner, Richard felt a little self-conscious. "To keep him warm, of course."

"And pretty," the little girl added with far more approval.

Pretty? He would have to apologize to Wally later.

Mrs. Reeves turned to him. "Do join us for tea, Richard. It is the tea I was given at Brockwell Court, but we are happy to share."

"Thank you, but I shan't stay. I only wanted to see if there was anything you needed."

Mother and daughter exchanged a look. Then Mrs. Reeves managed an unconvincing smile. "Not a thing. But I do thank you for your call."

Later, in the Brockwell Court drawing room, Richard flopped into a cushioned armchair with a book.

Timothy and Rachel came in. She picked up the stack of music he'd purchased. "Thank you, Richard."

"You are very welcome."

The others gathered. Arabella looked remarkably pretty in a pale blue evening gown, while Penelope and Horace looked as eager about the caroling as Richard felt. Murray, however, hummed to himself as he perused the music. Rachel must have coerced him into singing as well.

Rachel passed around the sheets of music while Justina spread hers on the pianoforte, Mr. Ashford smiling down at her all the while.

"You will sing with us, won't you, Richard?" his sister asked.

He raised his book as though a shield. "No. But I will listen and alert you if anyone is off-key, including the accompanist." He winked at her.

"Oh no," his brother said. "If you don't sing, you lose all right to criticize those who do. Not all of us have been blessed with the beautiful voice my wife has."

"Thank you, my dear," Rachel said. "What matters is to sing from the heart."

Horace nodded. "Though the right words and notes would not go unappreciated either."

Rachel looked from face to face. "Just do your best."

"I shall," Penelope said. "But be prepared for a 'joyful noise.'"

Horace chuckled, and Arabella smiled encouragement to her sister. Nicholas, he noticed, remained as near to the pianoforte, and his sister, as possible.

Justina struck the starting notes for each part.

Rachel said, "Ready?" and led out on the first line of "While Shepherds Watched Their Flocks by Night."

The others joined in, singing:

> "While shepherds watch'd their flocks by night,
>   All seated on the ground,
> The Angel of the Lord came down,
>   And Glory shone all around. . . ."

When they'd finished, his brother turned to Richard with a wry grin. "Well, what is your verdict?"

"Be glad you have other talents, Tim. That's all I'll say about you." Richard glanced at Arabella. Despite himself, he acknowledged, "But Miss Awdry has a lovely voice." Since she had already made it clear she had no interest in him, he felt there was little risk in being pleasant to her.

"Thank you, Mr. Brockwell," she said, turning quickly to his friend. "And I noticed Mr. Murray here is an excellent tenor."

Murray blushed and looked down. "Thank you. You can take the boy out of the boys' choir, but . . ." He left off with a shrug.

It was on the tip of Richard's tongue to add *And Penelope is an excellent bass*, but he thought the better of it.

Instead, he said, "Poor Murray. Still waiting for our voice to change, are we?" Richard grinned at his friend.

Murray quipped in turn, "Careful, or I'll start making you pay for all the books I lend you."

"Ah—touché. I shan't say another word against you. You have earned my silence and respect forever in a single blow."

Rachel interrupted, her words both an admonition and the next song title, "God *rest ye* merry, gentlemen."

They went on to practice a few more hymns and carols. Richard remained quiet after that, and although he did not intend to, his ears picked out Arabella's voice from the others'. His gaze strayed often to her lovely profile, but he determinedly turned a page of his book and pretended to read.

Later, after the others left the room, Justina lingered. "Why won't you sing with us?" she asked.

"Me? Caroling? I would be ruined socially, my masculinity doubted forever."

Justina snorted. "This from a grown man who dresses his dog like himself? I sincerely doubt you are really concerned about preserving your manliness."

"Ah! You are growing older and your tongue sharper. Your season with me in London did some good after all." He smirked.

"Be serious. Why won't you?"

"Because I don't wish to."

"Don't be such a humbug, Richard."

He tweaked her nose. "You may as well tell a tiger to change its stripes for spots."

CHAPTER

FIVE

On Sunday, most of the others went to church, but Richard stayed in bed, Wally asleep beside him. When the bells of St. Anne's woke him, he opened a book and read, willing Pickering to appear with coffee. But Pickering had apparently gone to church as well. *Traitor.*

Eventually Wally jumped down and scratched at the door. Heaving a sigh, Richard rose and began washing and dressing for the day.

Later that afternoon, most of the party gathered in the hall, dressed to go out and deliver Christmas baskets. His mother and Lady Lillian, however, opted to stay in and let the younger people brave the chill without them.

Rachel and Sir Timothy had composed a list of people they wished to give baskets to. Between her involvement with the library and the Ladies Tea and Knitting Society, and his position as magistrate, they knew most of the families in the parish.

They made it clear they did not expect everyone to help with the deliveries, aware some of their guests might not be comfortable visiting the homes of strangers, and some of them rather humble homes in the bargain. But most were willing to help, and Arabella was surprisingly eager.

When they finished adding the fresh bread to each basket, Richard took Rachel aside and asked, "Do you happen to have an extra basket?"

She looked up at him in surprise. "Yes, actually. Sadly, I learned one of the intended recipients passed away yesterday. Why?"

"There is someone in Wishford I'd like to give something to. Murray and I met him on the way here."

"The apprentice?"

"Yes. You remembered."

"That is very kind of you, Richard. How old is he?"

"Twelve or thirteen, I believe."

Rachel held up an index finger. "Give me one minute."

She returned with a cup and stringed ball game, carved of wood. "He might like this." She added it to the basket.

"Excellent idea. Thank you."

"Since you're going to Wishford, I might ask you to deliver a basket to the Mullins family, who live between here and there, if you don't mind."

He hesitated only a moment. "Very well."

"With whom shall I pair you? Mr. Murray? Miss Arabella?"

Richard considered. Deciding there was great pleasure to be had in talking with a beautiful woman who was not trying to snare him into matrimony, he replied, "Why not both? If you can spare the barouche-landau?"

"I think so, yes. I'll just ask Timothy to make sure he or Lady Barbara don't need it this afternoon."

Rachel turned to Justina and Mr. Ashford, who were ready to set out on their own together. "Let's all meet at the almshouse at three, shall we?"

Everyone agreed and departed in various directions—Sir Timothy and Rachel delivering baskets to the McFarland farm, to the midwife, and to the retired butler from Thornvale, and Justina and Nicholas taking baskets to the elderly sexton and two widowers.

Richard, Arabella, Murray, and Wally climbed into the barouche-landau, pulled by two horses and normally driven by a coachman sitting on the front box. But Horace begged to be allowed to drive, saying he was an excellent whip and often drove his father's chaise and four. The coachman acquiesced, and Penelope joined them, sitting next to Horace on the box.

They stopped first at the Mullinses' house, where Mr. and Mrs. Mullins and their several children received the overflowing basket with effusive gratitude and offers of spiced wine. Richard found he rather enjoyed being the bearer of gifts but felt sheepish to accept their gratitude. He deflected their praise, saying, "With the compliments of Sir Timothy and Lady Brockwell. We shall pass along your thanks to them."

He felt Arabella's gaze shift to him as he said it, but he kept his focus on Mr. and Mrs. Mullins. Arabella in turn began talking to their daughter, Sukey, and met her brothers, who ranged in age from six to sixteen. The eldest, Jeremy, mentioned he often worked for the Brockwells, especially during harvest time.

When their farewells were said, they next drove into Wishford and turned up a side street. Richard directed Horace to go around the churchyard, then pointed out the print shop. When they reached it, Horace and Penelope offered to stay with the horses and Wally. Richard descended first and gave Arabella a hand down. Murray followed on his own.

Richard led the way inside the shop, hoping his impulse would not prove to be a bad idea.

"Happy Christmas, Mr. Knock. Jamie. We come bearing gifts." He held the basket toward Jamie, but Knock swept in like a buzzard—arms spread and talons at the ready.

"That is very kind of you, Mr. Brockwell."

The heavy man grabbed the basket and eyed the contents with interest. Richard imagined he could almost see him drool. They ought to have waited until Mr. Knock was out of the shop. He cursed himself for not planning a better strategy.

Jamie gazed hopelessly at the basket. He seemed thinner and more careworn already.

"Wait, Mr. Knock." Richard kept his tone jovial. "These things are for Jamie to share as well. But this"—he extracted the cup-and-ball toy—"was chosen especially for the lad. What else are you partial to, Jamie? Perhaps the cheese?" He saw the boy looking at it longingly and handed the wedge to him.

Mr. Knock turned and carried the basket through a curtain to a back room, out of their reach. Richard guessed the cheese would be the only thing Jamie would be allowed to eat.

Richard gestured to his companions. Arabella lingered in the background, so he began with David. "Jamie, do you remember Mr. Murray?"

"Oh yes, sir. It was so kind of you to offer me your place in the coach."

"My pleasure, son. I see you still sport a few bruises from your fall."

Jamie looked down at his arms, then sent a frightened glance toward the back room.

"Yes, sir. Weren't nothing. I'm all right."

"Glad to hear it."

Richard turned to include Arabella. "And this is our friend, Miss Awdry. Miss Awdry, may I present Jamie Fleming."

"How do you do, Jamie." She came forward, smiling at the boy.

"I . . ." He stared at her, tongue-tied, clearly struck by her beauty. Richard couldn't blame him.

"A pleasure to meet you," Arabella added.

"You too, miss."

Wally, whom they'd left with Horace and Penelope, hopped down from the carriage and began scratching at the shop door, begging to be allowed inside.

"Someone is eager to see you," Richard said and opened the door.

Ignoring the others, Wally bounded straight for Jamie. The lad sank to his haunches and petted the dog, who licked his face. Then Wally caught the scent of something and headed for the stairs.

Returning from the back room, Mr. Knock caught him by his collar. "No, you don't. Nothing up there for you." He looked at the others. "What's this cur doing running loose in my shop?"

"Sorry, Mr. Knock." Richard picked up the dog. "Wally is mine, but he is fond of your apprentice here."

"Well, that makes one of us."

"No, Mr. Knock." With a glance that encompassed the others, Richard leveled a hard look at the man. "That makes four of us."

The man met the look, then narrowed his eyes. "Anything I can do for you, Mr. Brockwell? I do have an order to print before Christmas, if you don't mind?"

"Then we shall leave you to it. Enjoy your gift." Holding the door for Arabella and Murray, Richard left the shop, his stomach in knots.

"He isn't a very pleasant man, is he?" Arabella whispered.

"No."

Murray pointed out a faded *For Sale* sign on the window, among the other notices and advertisements. "That looks like it's been there a long time. No takers, apparently, and little wonder. I'm surprised a printer can make a go of it in a town this size."

Richard nodded his agreement. "Especially as rude as he is. My sister-in-law mentioned that most people go to the stationers in Salisbury even though it is farther, simply to avoid the man."

Arabella nodded. "I can well believe it."

Richard agreed. "A pity. Especially for Jamie."

At three, they met the others at the almshouse, each with a basket or two in hand for the residents.

They were met at the door by the almshouse matron, whom Rachel introduced as her friend, Mrs. Mennell. The matron in turn led them into a snug parlour off the entryway, where several elderly women and one man were all taking tea together. Richard would have handed over the baskets and gone, but Arabella pressed each person's hand, greeted them, and asked their names. She sat down next to a white-haired woman named Mrs. Russell who happily told her about her son, a sailor, and her great-granddaughter.

Standing there awkwardly, waiting for her to finish, Richard felt a bony hand take his. He looked down and found a kind-faced woman squinting up at him, thin grey plaits coiled and pinned atop her head.

"Good day, young man. Aren't you the handsome one." She grinned, then nodded toward Arabella across the room. "You've got a caring, gracious woman there. Hold on to her."

"Thank you, Mrs. . . . ?"

"Hornebolt."

"Thank you, Mrs. Hornebolt. I quite agree, but she is not mine to hold on to."

"Well, you had better get busy then. My vision isn't keen anymore, but I'd have to be blind not to see that you admire her."

Richard would have liked to contradict her but, to his surprise and chagrin, discovered he could not.

Returning to Brockwell Court, Arabella removed her gloves and bonnet and went upstairs to the room she shared with her sister. Penelope lingered downstairs with Mr. Bingley, having challenged him to a game of billiards. Although their mother deemed the game unladylike, society did not consider it improper for an unmarried lady to play in a private home, as long as she was not alone with a man. No fear of that—Lady Lillian was a diligent chaperone.

In the peace of the quiet bedchamber, Arabella reflected with pleasure on the events of the last two days—assembling gifts, singing carols, and delivering baskets with Mr. Murray and Richard while Horace drove and Penelope accompanied him. Her sister had enjoyed the outing, she knew, though for reasons different from hers.

She thought of Richard's awkward willingness to go to the Mullins farm, his polite humility with the family. And afterward, she had been surprised and impressed by his initiative and interaction with young Jamie Fleming. Too bad the boy's odious master had spoiled the otherwise jovial visit.

Richard Brockwell was a conundrum unto himself, she decided.

From his rude comments and indecorous teasing about sailor ditties, to behaving playfully with his nephew and generously with an apprentice he barely knew.

Something else confused her too. At the start of the house party, he had made every effort to avoid her, and when he could not, he'd insulted her and her sister instead. But his manner had changed. Not only had he been kindness itself to Pen lately, but to her as well, praising her singing and inviting her to accompany him and his friend in delivering baskets. She did not believe his character had really changed, so what explained it? Had he decided that, since she'd announced she had no interest in him, he could leave off trying to repulse her and be civil and even pleasant, without fearing she might misconstrue his kindness as more than it was?

Yes, that was likely it, and she would indeed take care not to read anything else in his polite deference. Certainly not admiration. Even so, she decided it would be wise to spend as little time as possible with Richard Brockwell.

CHAPTER

Six

The next morning, Richard and Wally dressed warmly and started down the corridor toward the back door.

Murray stepped out of the breakfast room and hailed him. "Going out? Would you mind some company?"

"Oh, I . . . Normally I would be glad of it, but . . ."

Murray winced. "Not regretting inviting me already, I hope."

"Not a bit of it. Just not sure you'd enjoy it. Thought I might pay a call on one of the widows who came here a few mornings ago. I knew her son, spent time with the family as a boy."

"One of the . . . what did you call them, mumpers? Kind of you. Well, I shall leave you to it."

"You know what? Do come along. It might help, actually."

"Very well, if you are sure. Let me fetch my coat and hat."

They set out together a few minutes later. As they walked along, Richard recalled his flippant words to Murray about pursuing Miss Awdry himself. Now he wanted to retract them. He told himself he was only trying to protect Murray from certain disappointment. He did not wish to see his friend get hurt.

"I have been thinking. You were right. Better not pursue Miss Arabella. That's a recipe for heartache."

His friend sent him a sidelong glance. "Is that a warning for me, or for you?"

The man was too clever for his own good. "For us both, I imagine."

Illogical though it might be, he didn't like the idea of Miss Arabella being courted by Murray—or by anyone else, for that matter.

Remembering Mrs. Reeves liked cured ham, Richard stopped by the Ivy Hill butcher's and bought a partial one and took the paper-wrapped parcel with him.

Nearing Honeycroft a short while later, Richard heard children's voices talking and laughing as they ran through the woods in some game.

Glancing at Murray, Richard explained, "Mrs. Reeves's grandchildren."

"Ah."

They reached the garden gate, and Richard saw his friend's eyes widen in surprise as he studied the rather dilapidated cottage.

"You spent time here growing up?"

"I did indeed."

The front door opened, and Susanna appeared, calling in a cheerful voice, "Peter! Hannah! Time to come inside."

Murray's gaze fixed on her. "That is no grandmother."

"No, that is her daughter, Susanna Evans."

"She is lovely."

"Yes."

He felt his friend's gaze shift to him, studying his profile. Perhaps bringing the observant man along had not been a good idea after all.

As Richard stepped through the gate, Susanna noticed him, and her expression hardened. "Mr. Brockwell. I told you, we don't need any—"

"Mrs. Evans, please allow me to introduce my friend, Mr. Murray." He turned, revealing his friend behind him.

"Oh." She faltered. "I did not realize." She managed a smile. "How do you do."

Murray bowed. "A pleasure to meet you, Mrs. Evans."

Richard lifted the parcel. "We've brought a little something for your mother. Is she here?"

"She is, yes, but she is feeling rather poorly today, I'm afraid."

"I am sorry to hear it. Shall I send for Dr. Burton?"

"No, we cannot . . . That is, we don't need a doctor. Mamma has a cold. That's all. I am sure it is nothing serious. But thank you for stopping by."

"Very well." Richard again held out the wrapped parcel, and for a moment Susanna made no move to accept it. "Just some ham," he said.

Reluctantly, she took it from him.

The children came running, eyes on the parcel. "What is it, Mamma?"

"Some ham for grandmother."

"Will she share?" the boy asked.

His sister nudged him. "Silly! She shares everything!"

Richard turned to go. "Do greet your mother for me," he said.

"I shall."

"And tell her I was sorry to miss meeting her," Mr. Murray added. "Richard has spoken so highly of her."

"Indeed I shall. Thank you, Mr. Murray."

He touched his hat brim. "Mrs. Evans."

On the walk back, Murray said, "Explain it to me, please. Why would a boy from Brockwell Court spend time in Honeycroft?"

"Because the Reeveses were the best of people. And their son, Seth, a dear friend of mine."

"And his sister?"

"She was . . . a friend of mine as well."

"There is more to it than that, I can see. But I shan't pry."

"Thank you."

Richard looked back over his shoulder. "Honeycroft may be humble, but when I was a lad the family kept it in spruce condition. Apparently, times have been difficult for Mrs. Reeves since her husband died. I wonder what might be done about that."

With that thought in mind, Richard and Murray walked into the village and down Potters Lane to the workshop of the local builders, the Kingsley Brothers.

The brick building had an extended roof over an open work area on one side and double doors to an enclosed workroom on the other. The sign above read:

KINGSLEY BROS.
MASONS, BUILDERS & CARPENTERS
PLANS MADE & ESTIMATES GIVEN

They entered through one of the broad double doors. Inside, a tall sandy-haired young man sawed boards to length. Wally sniffed eagerly at the wood shavings and sneezed.

Richard explained the situation at Honeycroft and asked Aaron Kingsley what inexpensive stopgap repairs might be made to the cottage before winter's damp and cold worsened.

"I can tell you exactly what it would entail and cost, for I gave Mrs. Reeves an estimate earlier this autumn. She didn't like it. Said she'd find someone else or do the repairs herself."

"Mrs. Reeves repair her own roof?" Richard echoed, voice rising with incredulity. "She's an elderly woman and not in good health. And I know for a fact she has hired no one. No doubt can't afford to. Truth is, I haven't much money either, but there must be something we can do."

The tall young man scratched his head. "Afraid we're not a charity, Mr. Brockwell. Materials cost money. And at all events, we're too busy to take on another project for at least a month."

"I see. Well, thank you anyway."

The two men walked out and continued down the street. Richard asked his friend, "Any carpentry or roofing experience?"

"Afraid not. You?"

"Zero."

Arabella put on her warmest pelisse and went out for a walk. She wanted to visit the Ivy Hill High Street and take a little exercise.

As she passed Potters Lane, Richard Brockwell and his friend came out of a builder's workshop. Richard had his dog on a leash. Even her brother, Cyril, would have left his dogs at home.

The men bowed and greeted her, and Richard said, "Good morning, Miss Awdry. What errand brings you out on this chilly day?"

So much for avoiding Richard Brockwell, she thought and replied, "I merely wished for a solitary walk."

"May we walk with you awhile?"

Murray hissed, "She said *solitary*, Richard."

Mr. Brockwell pressed a hand to his chest. "Pray, forgive me. Do you not want our company? I would never force my company on anyone when it is not wanted, except perhaps on my tailor."

Arabella hesitated. There was no polite way to refuse. "You are welcome to join me, if your dog is not too tired."

Mr. Brockwell smiled. "Not at all. We are all in fine fettle."

Did he have to be so handsome? She reminded herself that he was too much the dandy for her tastes, not to mention a reputed rake.

She turned and continued up the High Street, shifting her attention to his friend instead. "And how are you enjoying your time in Ivy Hill, Mr. Murray?"

"A great deal. It is far more peaceful than London. And the people far friendlier."

"I agree," she said. "Though there is something about London. So much happening. So much to see. Such a savory stew of different cultures and walks of life. Rich and poor, influential and voiceless . . ."

"Although, as with any stew, one must take the gristle along with the good," Murray added.

She nodded. "True. Even so, I find London compelling, fascinating, at times repulsive, but never dull."

"You have quite a way with words, Miss Awdry. Have you done any writing?"

"Goodness, no."

Had she imagined it, or did Mr. Brockwell roll his eyes at his friend's flattery?

When they reached the end of the street, a cold wind gusted up Ebsbury Hill and shivered down her neck.

In response, Richard murmured what seemed to be a bit of verse, "'See, Winter comes, to rule the varied year. . . .'"

She looked at him with interest. "Who wrote that?"

"The poet James Thomson, almost a hundred years ago." He sighed wistfully. "What must it be like, to write something people will still be reading and quoting a century from now."

"Instead of using it to wrap fish the next day?" Murray quipped.

"Exactly."

They turned right and started up Ebsbury Road. A woman walked in their direction, basket in hand, head bowed as if in thought. As she neared, Arabella saw that she was an attractive, dark-haired woman of perhaps thirty years, dressed in a simple gown and wool shawl.

Beside her, Richard's step faltered, then slowed. Arabella glanced over at him and noticed a strange tension in his profile.

The woman looked up. Her gaze flicked from her to Richard and back again, her expression inscrutable.

As she passed them, Richard and Mr. Murray bowed in acknowledgment. Murray said, "A pleasure to see you again, Mrs. Evans."

The woman dipped her head in return but made no reply.

After she passed by, Arabella said, "We could have stopped to talk with her, if you'd liked."

"No need. We have already spoken with her today."

Watching Richard's face, Arabella asked, "Do you know her well?"

"No. That is, we were acquainted when we were young."

They passed Church Street, Arabella intending to follow their current path out of the village. But Mr. Brockwell stopped. She turned around to see what had caused the delay.

He said, "Em . . . how far did you want to walk?"

"I am not sure." She gestured up the road. "I thought a brisk walk down country lanes might be just the thing before another rich meal."

"Well, you and Murray go ahead. Wally and I will head back." He gestured to the right along Church Street.

"Are you tired?"

"No. I usually avoid . . . That is, I think Wally is done in. Shorter legs, you see."

The dog however, strained against his master's hold, clearly eager to keep walking.

She glanced from man to man, Richard clearly uncomfortable and Mr. Murray quickly becoming so as the moments passed. Relenting, Arabella said, "Never mind. We'll all go back."

Both men looked relieved.

Richard had inwardly scoffed at Murray's flattering attentions to Arabella. Though could he blame the man? Pretty and intelligent and well spoken . . . It was enough to tempt any man of letters. His earlier description of her as a "silly, giggling thing," seemed completely unjust now. Had she changed so much, or did the fault lie with his own perceptions? His mother had told him he would find Miss Awdry much improved. And although it would gall him to admit it to anyone, she had been right. But intrigued with her as he might be, it was another female who stubbornly clung to Richard's thoughts for the rest of the day.

He tried to distract himself by playing billiards with Murray, who beat him handily for the first time in their long friendship. He even risked a visit to the nursery, hoping to see his nephew, only to be scolded by Nurse Pocket for speaking too loudly while Master Frederick napped.

Next he tried to lose himself in an old favorite book, but when an hour had passed without turning a page, he gave up and went and found his sister-in-law.

"Rachel, with your library and connections with village women, you probably know most everyone in Ivy Hill nowadays."

"Not everyone, but many people, yes."

"Then I have a question for you. How would one go about helping someone who doesn't want to be helped? Or rather is too proud to accept help . . . at least from me?"

Her blue eyes widened with interest. "Ah. And is this someone a female?"

"Why would you assume that? Never mind, yes. I see that gleam in your eye, sister, but I assure you this woman is an elderly widow, the mother of an old friend who has fallen on hard times. Her grown daughter and grandchildren have come home for Christmas, and I gather she is struggling to make ends meet for herself, let alone provide for three others."

"How old is this woman?"

"She must be five and fifty by now."

"I meant the daughter."

"Oh. My age. A recent widow with two children." He studied her face. "I see what you are thinking, but I promise you I have no nefarious designs on this woman, and she wisely wants nothing to do with me."

"How old are her children?"

"What does that matter?"

"It matters."

"I am no good at estimating ages, but if I had to guess, I would say the boy is about eight and the girl perhaps four or five."

"And could the older woman watch the children, so her daughter could work?"

"I assume so. Though apparently her mother's health is not all it should be at the moment."

"And their names?"

When he hesitated, she planted her hands on her hips. "How can I help someone if I don't know whom we are talking about?"

"Very well, but don't tell them I sent you or they'll rebuff you. And tread lightly. If the daughter gets a whiff of charity being offered, she'll dig in her heels. She is proud, as I said."

"As someone who used to refuse help for pride's sake, I understand completely and will proceed with utmost discretion. Their names?"

"Susanna Evans—that's her married name. Her mother is Mrs. Reeves."

"The beekeeper?"

"That was her husband's trade, primarily. After his death, Mrs. Reeves carried on as best she could until recent ill health prevented her."

"I see."

"Honeycroft is the name of their small property. Do you know where it is?"

Rachel squinted. "I am not certain."

"What about . . . Bramble Cottage?"

Rachel stilled. "Yes, I do. Though I am surprised you know of it."

For a moment they held one another's gazes. Then he looked away first. He said, "From there, you cross the road and walk through a grove of plum and cherry trees. I'd say you can't miss it, but you can. I stumbled upon it only by accident years ago. Though at this time of year, you can see the roof through the mostly bare tree branches."

"Very well," said Rachel. "Leave it to me."

On Monday evening, Rachel left her houseguests in Timothy and Justina's care, donned her coat and bonnet, and went downstairs. As she lingered in the hall to pull on her gloves, Miss Arabella Awdry approached her.

"And where are you off to, if that is not prying?"

"Not at all. I am going to the meeting of our local women's society."

The pretty woman's eyes lit up. "And what sorts of things does the society do? Is it a church charity guild?"

"Not exactly. It is called the Ladies Tea and Knitting Society, and is attended mostly by women involved in local businesses of one kind or another."

The interest on Miss Awdry's face faded. "Tea and knitting? How—" she struggled for a word—"pleasant."

Rachel grinned. "It sounds rather mundane, I know. I hesitated to attend myself at first, and now don't get to as many meetings as I would like since having Frederick, but I promise you they do far more than needlework and drinking tea." Rachel paused. "Would you like to come along? Guests are welcome, and you might find it interesting."

"I would like to see what a meeting is like. The others are play-ing whist, but I don't care for cards. And I confess, idleness makes me restless. Give me just a minute to find my cloak."

Together, they walked up Potters Lane and into the village hall a short while later. There, Rachel introduced Miss Awdry to her dear friends, Mercy Kingsley and Jane Locke.

"Ah yes, I remember you both," Arabella said. "A pleasure to see you again."

"And you, Miss Awdry," Jane said. "You were only a girl when last I saw you, and now you are a lovely young woman."

"Thank you. Though not so young anymore. I am six and twenty."

"As ancient as that?" Jane teased. "Oh, to be so young again." She tilted her head to the side in thought. "Actually, that's not true. I am happy as I am and wouldn't trade my life for all the youth in the world."

"Nor I," Mercy agreed.

Rachel said, "Mercy and her husband operate a charity school between Ivy Hill and Wishford."

Arabella's face brightened. "Oh! We passed it on the way to Brockwell Court. I noticed the sign." She quoted, "'The Fairmont Boarding & Day School. Pupils accepted, regardless of ability to pay.'"

Mercy smiled. "Very good."

"I think it is wonderful what you are doing, Mrs. Kingsley."

"Thank you. We are enjoying the school immensely, though managing it is not without its trials and challenges."

Arabella nodded. "As is the case with any worthwhile endeavor."

"True. We feel blessed to be able to educate children, especially those who would otherwise not be educated at all."

"I applaud you," Arabella said earnestly. "I have little experience, but is there anything I could do to help while I am here? If you ever need a volunteer for anything, please do let me know."

"That is very kind of you, Miss Awdry."

"If only one of us had a harp," Rachel said. "Arabella plays beautifully. She might have given a little Christmas concert for the children."

"I did not bring ours along, unfortunately," Arabella said. "It is rather cumbersome to transport."

Mercy's eyes brightened. "Actually, I discovered an old harp in the Fairmont attic."

"Is that old harp still there?" Jane asked.

Rachel explained to Arabella, "Jane grew up in Fairmont House."

Jane nodded. "The harp was my grandmother's. I am not certain what its condition would be after all this time, but she always took excellent care of it."

"Well, I will ask Joseph and Mr. Basu to bring it downstairs," Mercy said. "You are welcome to come over and see what you think of it. If it won't suit, you could always read to the younger children instead. They are learning to read themselves, of course, but it is so good for them to be read to, I believe."

"I would happily do so. Just name a time."

"Perhaps some evening after dinner, if you are free."

"Gladly."

Seemingly eager to shift the attention from herself, Mercy turned to Jane. "And Jane and Mr. Locke are the owners of a prospering horse farm on the outskirts of Ivy Hill."

"Oh?" Arabella's fair brows rose. "I thought I heard you were an innkeeper?"

Jane chuckled. "I was, indeed. But my former brother-in-law

fills that role now. I love horses and working beside my new husband, so it is a mutually beneficial arrangement all around. Our son, Jack Avi, is growing up to be quite the horseman as well."

"Congratulations. I am afraid I know little about horses," Arabella said, "but my brother and sister do. In fact, my sister mentioned being eager to visit Locke stables, though I didn't realize your connection to the place. Apparently, she and my brother are interested in a pair of hunters."

"They are welcome to visit at any time."

Several other women came forward to greet the newcomer, the Miss Cooks admiring the lacework on her sleeves, and Mrs. Klein, who mentioned she regularly tuned the Broadmere pianoforte, respectfully greeted the young woman, passing along her compliments to her family.

Then Mercy called the meeting to order. They discussed plans to bring Christmas cheer to the almshouse and a few other struggling families. The vicar's wife gave a report on the church charity guild and her family's plans to host a buffet meal for anyone without somewhere else to go on Christmas Day. Several women offered to help prepare food or serve.

When Mercy asked for any other business, Rachel stood. "It has come to my attention that Mrs. Reeves is not in good health and is struggling to get by, especially at this time of year."

Mrs. O'Brien said, "I thought her daughter came home for Christmas?"

Rachel nodded. "She has come home, perhaps permanently. Her husband died, and she has two young children to care for. It makes sense for Mrs. Reeves and her daughter to pool their resources and share a home, but apparently Honeycroft has fallen into disrepair."

Mrs. Burlingame said, "She sold no honey at market this year. Mrs. Craddock had to go to Salisbury to buy some for the bakery."

Mrs. Snyder tsked. "So no income and poor health. No wonder Mrs. Reeves is in decline and her cottage too."

"Has anyone heard of any positions her daughter might take on to help support the family?" Rachel asked.

Around the room, heads slowly shook in the negative.

"I have been thinking of hiring a nurserymaid to assist our nurse," Rachel said. "Miss Pocket is rather elderly and has not a lot of energy for keeping up with Frederick. I don't know if Susanna Evans would be interested in such a situation, but I thought I might offer it to her, if any of you might vouch for her character?"

"Oh yes, Susanna was always a good girl," Mrs. Burlingame said. "Though I have not seen much of her in recent years, after she married and moved away."

"You might ask your brother-in-law, my lady," Mrs. Snyder said. "He was a friend to Seth Reeves, Susanna's brother."

"Was he indeed? How unusual," Charlotte Cook said. "Wouldn't expect a Brockwell to befriend a Reeves. Pray do not be offended, my lady."

"I am not."

"If you have not met her," Mrs. Barton said, "I wonder how you learned of her situation?"

Remembering Richard's plea to keep his name out of it, she said, "We saw Mrs. Reeves on St. Thomas Day, and she looked rather peaky. I heard the rest in passing."

Becky Morris asked, "If Susanna finds work, will her mother be in fit condition to care for the children while she's away? Would you require Susanna to live in?"

"As Nurse Pocket lives in, I think we could manage perfectly well with a nurserymaid's help during the day."

Mrs. Burlingame nodded. "Perhaps some of us might make up a schedule to call on Mrs. Reeves regular-like. Make sure she and the children have all they need while Susanna's away at the manor. The little 'uns ain't so little anymore, and the boy's old enough to keep an eye on his sister, should Mrs. Reeves need to rest or whatnot. I can stop by on my route."

Charlotte Cook said, "Judy and I can pay a call on Monday afternoons. Our shop is closed then."

Around the room, other women offered to visit weekly or bi-weekly as needed, and the rotation was agreed upon.

Rachel smiled at one and all. "Thank you, ladies. I will call on Susanna Evans tomorrow and offer her the post. I will let you know if she accepts."

Later, when Rachel and Arabella walked home together, Rachel asked her, "What did you think of the meeting?"

"Very interesting. I like how the women help one another, especially those less fortunate. It reminds me of my Aunt Genevieve's work in London. She is most philanthropic and is personally involved with two charities while giving money to several others. I want to be like her, and join her in her work one day, if I can."

"Commendable."

Arabella looked at her, likely studying her face for censure. "I don't say it to impress you or to boast. Heaven knows I have done nothing worth boasting about in my life so far. Oh, the constraints placed on gently bred females!"

"Your mother does not support your charitable leanings?"

"No. She does not approve of her sister's bluestocking ways either. And in turn, Aunt Gen thinks my mother a vain and silly woman more interested in impressive marriages for her children than in helping the poor."

"I see." Rachel personally believed a woman could be a dutiful wife and mother *and* help the less fortunate at the same time, but she resisted the temptation to lecture. Instead, she took the young woman's arm and said kindly, "Well, I believe you will find Christmastide in Ivy Hill to be most . . . enlightening."

The next morning, Rachel and Timothy prepared to set off for Honeycroft together, he wearing his greatcoat and she a fur-trimmed mantle. Recalling Richard saying Susanna was too proud to accept charity, she decided not to bring any gifts of food on this occasion.

Since she did not know exactly where the cottage was, and Richard said the way passed through a lonely wood, Timothy had offered to accompany her. Rachel feared a baronet's presence might make Mrs. Reeves and her daughter uncomfortable, but Timothy reminded Rachel that Frederick was his child too, and he had a vested interest in interviewing the potential nurserymaid who would share the care of his dear son.

"Very well, my love." Rachel ran her hand over his lapels. "But do try not to look so . . . tall and handsome and intimidating."

"I shall do my best." He grinned and kissed her cheek.

"And I don't know if she will even want the post. She might see it as beneath her. She isn't exactly a young girl. Are you sure you have not heard of any other available positions?"

"Nothing except for a fishmonger's assistant in Wishford. And I trust a place in Brockwell Court will be more appealing than that."

"True."

Together they drove in Timothy's curricle down the Brockwell

Court drive, past the inn, and up the High Street. Soon they left the village lanes behind and neared Bramble Cottage, where their relationship had been tested and strengthened before their marriage.

"I wonder how Mrs. Haverhill is getting on in Brighton," Rachel mused.

"I assume she is doing well and plans to remain there," Timothy replied, "for the agent told me she intends to sell Bramble Cottage outright, when she only let it out before."

"I see. Well, I miss her, but I am glad she is doing well."

"As am I."

Per Richard's directions, they passed Bramble Cottage, then turned off the road and followed an overgrown path through a grove of bare-branched trees.

Soon Rachel saw a broken chimney, thatched roof, and garden wall. Timothy alighted first, secured the horses to a post, and helped her down. Entering through the listing garden gate, they walked on a path bordered by brown grass and weeds, past beehives in disarray, and followed the sound of wood chopping to the back of the house. There they found a dark-haired woman in her late twenties, axe in hand, splitting logs, a wool muffler wrapped around her head and a pair of worn gloves on her hands that were clearly too big for her.

She turned at their approach and slowly lowered the axe, body and expression tightening as if anticipating bad news.

"Good day," Rachel began. "You are Mrs. Evans, I assume?"

She nodded, eyes wary.

"We are Sir Timothy and Lady Brockwell."

The woman's gaze rested on her husband. "I would know you anywhere, sir."

Timothy hesitated. "Have we met?"

"Not formally."

Rachel let that pass, guessing the woman referred to Timothy's resemblance to his brother. She said, "We were hoping to talk to you about a possible situation. If you are willing to consider it?"

She frowned. "Did Richard send you? I told him we don't need help."

"Actually, we are the ones in need of help," Rachel gently explained. "We need a nurserymaid for our young son, Frederick."

"I have two children of my own."

"Yes, so I've heard."

"Who told you that?"

"I am a member of the local Ladies Tea and Knitting Society. Mrs. Burlingame and Mrs. Snyder speak highly of you and your mother."

The back door opened, and an elderly woman, shawl around her shoulders, appeared on its threshold.

"Susanna, invite our guests inside, for heaven's sake. It's too cold to stand talking out here."

"Oh. Forgive me. Would you like to come inside? It's a little warmer in there."

Her reserve belied her invitation, but Rachel accepted. "Yes, thank you."

In the cottage's main room, which clearly served as both dining room and parlour, a small smoky fire burned low in the grate. One of the windows had been boarded over. The house was, as Susanna had said, a little warmer but not warm enough.

Mrs. Reeves covered a cough with a gloved hand, then smiled at them.

"Sir Timothy, a pleasure to see you, sir. And Lady Brockwell, welcome. I could only wish our home were less humble, or that I had some refreshment to offer you. All I have are the dainties we received from you, and it doesn't seem right to offer those back to you."

"Don't give it another thought, Mrs. Reeves. We shan't stay long. We were hoping to interest your daughter in a situation at Brockwell Court, if she would like one."

Susanna shook her head. "I don't want charity."

"Who said anything about charity? A nurserymaid to Miss Pocket will work hard and be tested, I don't doubt. And as much as we love our Frederick, looking after him requires a great deal of effort."

"I couldn't. I have my own children and Mother to look after."

"Oh, come my dear," Mrs. Reeves protested. "I can look after myself and my own grandchildren. They are not babes anymore."

"Nurse Pocket lives in," Rachel added, "so we were thinking yours could be a daily situation. You could come home at night, say after Frederick's dinnertime?"

Mrs. Reeves nodded. "That sounds very reasonable, my lady."

The children came in. The boy of about eight and the girl of four or five, as Richard had described. Their grandmother urged, "Come and meet Sir Timothy and Lady Brockwell."

The two came forward, shy but polite.

"Good day, sir. Madam," the boy said.

The girl stood beside her brother, half-hidden behind his back, her large eyes fastened on Rachel. "You look like a princess."

Rachel smiled at her. "I am not a princess, I assure you, my dear. But thank you for the compliment."

Susanna placed one hand on the boy's shoulder and the other on the girl's head. "I don't mind hard work, and I can't deny we need the money. If the position were anywhere else, I would not hesitate. But to work in Brockwell Court . . ."

She was thinking of Richard, Rachel guessed. Just what had transpired between the two? She glanced at Timothy and noticed a slight frown crease his brow. Was he aware of their history, whatever it was? She guessed not.

To assure Susanna that Richard would not be in residence for long, Rachel said, "As it is the Christmas season, we do have a house full of guests at present, which is in part why we could use more help, as I cannot be with Frederick as much as I would like. But after Epiphany, things will quiet down. It will just be Frederick, me, and Sir Timothy, his mother, sister, and of course the other staff members."

Sir Timothy named the wages he thought fair.

Susanna's mouth parted, a half laugh, half protest escaping her. "More than fair, but—"

"She accepts," Mrs. Reeves blurted, giving her daughter a little nudge. "When would you like her to start?"

Remembering Mrs. Reeves was partial to grayling, which were in season in December, Richard and Wally drove to the fishmongers in Wishford and bought two fresh fish, planning to drop off the paper-wrapped parcel on his way home. He also stopped briefly at the printers. Jamie looked up hopefully, but Mr. Knock waved Richard away. "Can't stop to talk, Mr. Brockwell. One more job to finish before we close for Christmas."

Insolent man. Sending a smile in Jamie's direction, Richard reluctantly took his leave.

Richard drove the back roads to Ivy Hill, and as he neared the village, he saw a female figure trudging up the hill, burlap sack and basket in arms. A small boy walked beside her, carrying a second bag.

The boy glanced over his shoulder, and Richard recognized him as Susanna's son, Peter.

Richard called, "Susanna! Em, Mrs. Evans! May I give you a lift home?"

She glanced over but kept on walking. "No, thank you, Mr. Brockwell."

"Mamma . . ." the boy whispered loudly. "This is heavy."

"Yes, please do allow me to help," Richard offered, halting the horses beside them.

"We don't need help, Mr. Brockwell."

The boy's eyebrows raised, and he repeated plaintively, "*Mamma . . .*"

Susanna turned to him. "Oh very well. Thank you, Mr. Brockwell. A ride home would be most appreciated . . . for Peter's sake."

"For Peter's sake. Understood. Slide over, Wally."

They stowed their parcels on the floor and climbed up onto the cushioned seat, Peter sitting on his mother's lap, Wally snug between them.

"We went for supplies in Wishford," Susanna explained. "Prices are better there than at Prater's. I want to make sure Mother is well supplied before I start working. Never realized how heavy flour, suet, and turnips could be."

Richard told his horses to walk on, and the curricle set off again. Awkward silence followed. He knew from Rachel that she had offered Susanna a position. He wondered how his old friend felt about it and supposed she would not relish the notion of working in his family's home.

As they rode along, she sent him a sidelong glance. "I suppose I have you to thank for the job offer."

"Not at all. I had no idea my sister-in-law needed a nursery-maid."

She sent him a skeptical, sidelong glance. "The last thing I want is a situation at Brockwell Court. But we need the money, and Lady Brockwell hinted you would not be staying long. Is that true?"

"Yes."

"Good."

He winced at her brusque tone, then asked politely, "When do you start?"

"Boxing Day. They said I could wait till after, but this way Nurse Pocket can have some time off."

"Kind of you."

She nodded curtly and stared straight ahead.

He glanced at her strained profile and regret pinched his heart. Once upon a time, she had looked him directly in the eye, expression open and warm and . . . loving.

He said quietly, "I am sorry, you know."

For a moment she did not respond, and he wondered if she'd heard or if she was deliberately snubbing him.

Then she replied in equally low tones, "No, I don't know that."

Peter, little forehead furrowed, looked one from to the other. "Sorry for what?"

Richard thought, *For letting things go too far and then leaving without a word* . . . But aloud he said only, "Oh, many things. For not visiting your grandmother earlier, for example. I am very glad you three have come to visit now."

"We are not visiting, not really," Peter replied. "We've come to live here. We had to give up our old place. Couldn't pay the rent."

"Shh. That is enough, Peter. Mr. Brockwell does not need to hear all of our problems." To Richard, she amended, "While my husband lived, we were perfectly comfortable. I don't want you to think he did not provide for us. He was put on half pay after he was injured, and with the doctor's bills and all . . . things became difficult. More so when he passed on."

"No pension?"

She shrugged. "We married without his commanding officer's approval, and as he was not an officer. . . . No. Nothing to speak of."

"I am sorry to hear it."

She glanced significantly toward her son. "But we will be all right. Nothing to worry about. God has always watched over us, and He always will. You do believe that, Peter, do you not?"

"Yes, Mamma."

Richard wondered if she sincerely believed it, evidence to the contrary, or if she only said the words to reassure her son. Parents, he knew, sometimes said things to appease their children, whether true or not.

Then again, he thought, he himself had enjoyed a life of ease, yet his own belief in God's provision was weak.

As they neared the turnoff to Honeycroft, Richard darted a look toward Bramble Cottage in the distance, and his chest tightened. He quickly averted his gaze. He was glad he did not have to pass too close to it to deliver Susanna home. He'd done his best to avoid that place for years and saw no reason to change now.

As if reading his thoughts, Susanna said softly, "She has moved away, you know. Over a year ago."

He had not known, but he made do with a nod. The tension gathering in his chest eased.

When they reached the garden gate, Richard slowed the horses and Susanna gathered her shopping. Wally began sniffing at the wrapped fish he'd all but forgotten about.

"Thank you for reminding me, Walt."

He handed the parcel to Peter. "Grayling for your grandmother. Though I trust there's enough to share."

"Thank you, sir."

Susanna nodded stiffly. "Yes, thank you, Mr. Brockwell. Though you really shouldn't have."

"I wish there was more I could do."

She dipped her head, sadness clouding her pretty features. "And I wish I could believe you."

That afternoon they all gathered in the great hall to help decorate Brockwell Court. Christmas Eve was the traditional day to put up the decorations that would be taken down twelve days later. The gardener and groundsman had already gathered holly, ivy, and fragrant cuttings of rosemary, bay, and Scots pine. Rachel and her lady's maid supplied twine, scissors, silk, and gold paper.

The servants set up a large makeshift table in the open hall, and everyone found a spot and set to work. With the housekeeper, Mrs. Dean, instructing them and Lady Barbara supervising, they created long garlands by intertwining holly, pine boughs, and ivy. The men wound the garlands around the columns supporting the entrance porch and down the long stately staircase. Then Justina and Arabella added festive ribbon bows.

They dressed the mantels and windows with more garlands of evergreens. And Lady Barbara draped a garland of Christmas roses around the portrait of Sir Justin, her late husband. Then the women made daintier garlands of rosemary and bay branches to decorate the dining room table and chandelier.

Richard decided to create his own favorite decoration: a kissing bough, made of holly, ivy, and mistletoe. Normally his mother frowned on the use of mistletoe with its pagan origins, but this year she made no complaint, agreeable to anything that might spark romance between the gathered young people. He hung it in the archway of the drawing room.

Soon the house was filled with the tangy smells of pine, rosemary, and bay leaves, along with the savory scents coming from the kitchen.

Richard found himself enjoying the simple pleasure of working with his hands, but his mind kept returning to Jamie Fleming and the odious Mr. Knock. What sort of Christmas would they be having? Richard doubted it would be a cheerful one. He decided he had a letter to write and an errand to do.

The decorating done, Richard excused himself. "Pray pardon me, ladies. I feel the need to ride off on an errand."

"Richard, no. Not on Christmas Eve," his mother protested. "I know you plan to while away the hours in the public house, but we need you here."

He pressed his chest. "You wound me, Mamma. I have no intention of whiling away the entire evening in the public house, though thank you for the suggestion. Perhaps a pint or two of Christmas cheer would not go amiss."

"Richard, you are incorrigible."

"Thank you. It is one of my best qualities."

With Pickering's help, Richard changed into riding clothes, donned his greatcoat, and strode out to the stables. A short while later, he rode past The Bell Inn and down the hill toward Wishford on horseback.

The sun set around four in late December, so already the sky was darkening. He rode past candlelit homes and frosty fields, scared up a pheasant, and continued into the neighboring village. Reaching the print shop, Richard dismounted and tied the horse to a nearby post. From the look of the shop, he would not be staying long enough to bother taking his horse to the livery. The shop windows were dim, and when he tried the door, he found it latched. Not surprising, Richard supposed, that the shop would be closed on Christmas Eve.

Richard stepped back and looked at the windows above. Dark there as well. Apparently no one was at home. Had the man taken his apprentice with him, wherever he went to celebrate the holiday?

Then he saw an upper curtain flick to one side. Was that a face behind the glass?

"Jamie?" Richard called.

A moment later the window creaked open. "Shop's closed for Christmas, sir."

"So I see. What are you doing up there in the dark?"

"Just waiting, sir. Mr. Knock told me not to burn any candles. Dear, they are."

"Where is he?"

"Gone to his brother's in Grimstead."

"And what are you supposed to do while he's away? Sit there in the dark?"

"I'm to watch over things."

"Could you come down here, please? I am getting a crick in my neck talking up at you."

"Very well. Though I am supposed to keep the door locked."

"I am not a thief. Come down."

A minute later, the door unlatched and tentatively opened. If possible, the lad looked thinner than the last time he'd seen him.

"Has he left you anything to eat and drink?"

"Oh . . . I'll be all right, sir. There's a bit of bread and a few apples."

"But it's Christmas!"

The boy shrugged. "I don't expect anything. Only an apprentice, after all. Never really celebrated Christmas. Though at the orphan home we had a turkey and bread pudding. Delicious."

"Let me understand you. You are to sit alone in the dark for days with nothing but a scrap of bread and a few wizened apples?"

"Well, it's not dark all day."

"What about the basket we brought?"

"Took it with him."

"And the cheese?"

"I ate some of it. I hid the rest, but it found it."

"What do you mean 'it'?"

The boy shuddered. "The big rat that lives in the garret."

Richard pressed his eyes closed and barely restrained an epithet.

"No. It won't do." He shook his head. "Get your coat. You're coming with me."

The boy's mouth fell slack. "I'm not to leave, sir. If I did, Mr. Knock would punish me, and I don't want that."

"Grimstead is miles from here. When is he expected back?"

"He didn't say exactly. Didn't want me to get any ideas about running off."

"Never mind. The sign on the door says closed till December twenty-seventh."

"But if he should come back early and find me gone . . ." The boy shivered.

"Leave it to me. I shall write a note for him, just in case. Telling him I gave you no choice but to come with me. Will that do?"

"Maybe."

"Come, Jamie. I promise you mince pies and every good thing if you accompany me."

The boy hesitated. "But . . . can I trust you, sir?"

"Ah. You are wise to be cautious. Life has no doubt taught you to be wary of strangers. But we are not strangers any longer. And you met my friends Murray and Miss Awdry. Between us, we will make sure no harm comes to you."

"Where would you take me?"

"Brockwell Court. Where I grew up. It's only a few miles from here."

"But they can't want me there. Not in a place like that. Or . . . do you need help? Is that it?"

"Yes, we need a great deal of help eating the feast our cook is preparing. If you think you are equal to the task."

"Well . . . if you truly don't think they'd mind—and have enough to spare, that is."

"Indeed we do. And don't worry, I won't make you come upstairs with my lot. Boring, highbrow toffs. But our housekeeper is a good sort, as is Pickering. You met him too. The older man?"

"And your dog, sir?"

"Yes, Wally will be delighted to see you again."

Jamie looked down at his stained, grubby clothes. "I am not fit for a mine shaft, let alone a manor house."

Richard said gently, "If they let me in, they'll let in anyone."

The lad looked up, hope sparking in his eyes. "May I have five minutes to wash my face and put on my clean shirt?"

"Yes, by all means."

While he was gone, Richard wrote the note to Mr. Knock, explaining he had insisted Jamie join them at Brockwell Court for Christmas and promising to return him.

A few minutes later, Jamie trotted downstairs, face clean, hair slicked back, coat buttoned, and flat cap in hand.

"Do you mind riding behind me on the horse?" Richard asked.

"I . . . don't mind, though I have not done so before. I hope I don't fall off."

"We'll take it slow."

Twenty or thirty minutes later, man and boy rode at a leisurely pace up the Brockwell Court drive, past the shaped hedges and fountain. Candles shown from the windows, and the greenery around the columns gave the house a welcome warmth. Even Richard could not fail to appreciate the manor's appeal.

Jamie asked in wonder, "You grew up here, sir?"

"Well, *if* I've grown up, here is where it happened."

"It's a beauty. And so big."

Richard could not disagree.

They took the horse to the stable, where the groom helped Jamie down, then took charge of the animal. Richard and the boy walked together toward the rear door. Jamie sent him an uncertain glance, removed his hat, and smoothed back his hair.

"All will be well. I promise," Richard assured him, and led him inside and belowstairs.

There they encountered the housekeeper. "Ah, Mrs. Dean. May I introduce to you Jamie Fleming. Jamie is an apprentice in Wishford. Jamie, this is Mrs. Dean, our esteemed housekeeper. I know it is a busy time, but I hope you will make him welcome."

The woman blinked, clearly surprised by the request. "To be

sure, your young friend is welcome. But might we . . . em . . . discuss the arrangements?"

"Ah, of course. Just give us a few moments, Jamie."

"Yes, sit yourself down, young man. Be comfortable."

Following the housekeeper into her sitting room, Richard explained the lad's predicament—left to shift for himself on Christmas with barely enough food to keep a mouse alive.

She shook her head, nostrils flared. "Never liked that Mr. Knock."

"Needless to say, the boy doesn't expect to join the party upstairs. That would frighten him to death. But a few good meals and a warm cot somewhere for two nights?"

"Yes, we can manage that. I will speak to Mrs. Nettleton. And what about church tomorrow?"

"Oh. I had not thought of that. If he wants to go, very well, but we need not force him."

She smirked. "Are we talking about him or you?"

He chuckled. "Both of us."

"What is Christmas without going to church, Master Richard? The crib, the Christ child, the hymns . . ."

"As you think best, Mrs. Dean."

He turned to go, but she called him back. "May I say that it was kind of you, Mr. Brockwell."

He shrugged off the unfamiliar praise like a stranger's cloak.

"I did nothing. But I appreciate your help. And I know he will appreciate any kindness you show him."

Richard joined the others for dinner and smiled and nodded his way through the meal, but all the while wondered how Jamie was getting on belowstairs.

Afterward, instead of lingering over port with the gentlemen, he slipped back downstairs.

In the passage, he heard the cook talking to the housekeeper, and none too happily.

"Easy for him to take in a stray and then expect *us* to feed 'im and bed 'im down. The urchin will probably steal us blind in the middle of the night. What's the man up to? Never knew Master Richard to do a kind, selfless deed in his life. What's in it for him?"

"Nothing, as far as I know."

Mrs. Nettleton frowned and crossed beefy arms over an ample bosom. "Humph."

Richard turned from the door, deciding it was not the best time to make his presence known.

Upstairs, Timothy stood waiting for him in the hall.

"Wondered where you went. Looking in on your young guest?"

"Yes. How did you hear of it?"

"Mrs. Dean mentioned his arrival to me just before dinner. I must say I am as surprised as she was. Though perhaps I ought not have been, as Rachel mentioned you took a basket to the apprentice."

"Mrs. Nettleton doesn't seem too happy about an extra mouth to feed, but Mrs. Dean was gracious about it. I hope you don't mind?"

"I don't mind, though I do find it curious."

"So do I, in all honesty. But it seemed the right thing to do."

Timothy nibbled his lip. "He will have to go back, you know. There are strict laws about apprenticeships and severe penalties when they run off from their masters."

"I know." Dull dread filled Richard at the thought. "But it's only for Christmas."

His brother nodded. "As long as you both remember that."

Later that Christmas Eve, Justina announced it was time for dancing, and all heaved themselves to their feet to oblige her. Rachel had arranged for Mrs. Klein, the local piano tuner and an accomplished musician, to play for them.

The footmen moved the furniture from one end of the long room and rolled up the large Turkish carpet.

Justina called the first dance, and she and Mr. Ashford stood at the top of the set as lead couple. Before Richard could act, Horace

Bingley claimed Arabella, and Timothy and Rachel joined them, forming two facing lines for a longways dance.

Richard dutifully asked his mother to dance, but she waved him away, protesting she was too old and too full to dance, so he turned and asked Penelope instead.

She hesitated. "I don't mind sitting out if you'd rather not dance with me. I know you would rather dance with Arabella. And clearly Mr. Bingley does too."

Richard saw the disappointment written on the tall woman's face. "I am sure he will dance the next with you, and if he does not, he is more the simpleton than I believed him. Let's dance, Miss Awdry. Show them how it's done."

Penelope grinned. "I am willing if you are. But I must warn you, I have never been light on my feet."

"I consider myself duly warned." Richard gave a little bow and offered his arm, then together he and Arabella's sister joined the others.

When she saw her sister's smile and heard Pen and Richard talking and laughing together, Arabella's regard for Mr. Brockwell grew. She watched the two covertly as they danced. He moved with natural athletic grace, and when Pen made a wrong turn or collided with someone, he helped her recover with good humor and kindness, which impressed Arabella.

The couples completed a set of country dances, then paused to change partners.

Arabella wondered if Richard would ask her to dance and told herself it would be better if he did not. Better to keep her distance. She feigned interest in her fan, trying not to appear eager. Yet she could not deny her feelings for the man had started to change, her prejudice against him to soften. *Don't be swayed so easily*, she told herself. *Men don't change, do they? At least not that quickly. Guard your heart.*

He approached and asked, "May I have the next, Miss Arabella? Your sister survived dancing with me, after all."

She hesitated, searching his handsome face for sincerity or jest. Should she politely decline? Standing so near to him, she smelled his spicy shaving tonic and saw the warm light in his blue eyes. Her stomach tingled with anticipation, and her disloyal tongue replied, "With pleasure."

Horace and Penelope joined them, as did Rachel and Mr. Ashford, and Sir Timothy with Justina.

Mrs. Klein played the introduction of another country dance, and the four new couples took their places.

After balancing right and left, they turned and changed places. Mr. Brockwell took both of her hands in his, and together they moved around their neighbors. He looked steadily into her eyes as he did so, an admiring smile on his handsome face. Despite herself, she smiled back, enjoying his attention and the feeling of her hands in his. Finally, they joined four hands across and circled right, then left.

The simple pattern repeated, and each time Mr. Brockwell faced her or took her hands, his gaze held hers. He really was most attractive—elegant yet masculine, and so appealingly confident . . .

Near them, Penelope tripped on her own hem and stumbled. Horace reached out to steady her.

Pen's face reddened. "Sorry. I am no good at this."

"Not at all, Miss Awdry. You dance very . . . resolutely."

Penelope grinned at him, and the two danced on.

When the set ended, Mr. Brockwell offered Arabella his arm and escorted her across the room toward the waiting chairs. "You are a beautiful dancer, Miss Arabella. Not to mention a beautiful woman."

Her cheeks warmed with pleasure. She looked up into his beguiling blue eyes, thinking, *I could say something similar of you,* but she made do with a murmured, "Thank you."

The footman brought in punch, tea, and coffee, and they all paused to take refreshment, sitting on the clustered chairs and sofa, talking and laughing and catching their breath.

Arabella turned back to Richard, found his warm eyes fastened upon her, and wondered what it would be like to be married to such a man. She pushed aside the surprising thought, reminding herself of her plans to remain single and move to London. Besides, would a man like Richard Brockwell ever love a woman enough to honor his marriage vows and remain faithful to her alone for the rest of her life? She doubted it.

From her place at the end of the sofa, Justina leaned forward to ask, "You will go to church with us tomorrow, won't you, Richard? It is Christmas, after all."

He made a face. "I have not darkened the door of a church in years, except the occasional wedding or funeral."

Surprise flashed through Arabella. "Really? How sad."

He looked at her with interest. "Why sad?"

"How much you miss. The fellowship, the worship, the inspiring reminder of whose you are and why you are here on earth."

"The long, tedious sermons and repetitive prayers . . ."

Justina shook her head. "Don't say that. Mr. Paley is a dear, good man."

"Never said he wasn't. His sermons could do with a skilled editor—that's all I'm saying. Or is he paid by the word, as many writers are?"

"You're terrible," Justina scolded. "But you need not worry. He won't keep us overlong tomorrow. Not with Christmas dinner waiting."

Horace Bingley patted his stomach. "I hope you are right."

Later, when people were beginning to say their good-nights and depart for bed, Arabella turned to Richard once more and said quietly, "I sincerely hope you will join us tomorrow, Mr. Brockwell."

He looked at her, flattered but slightly wary at the same time.

On impulse, he nodded toward the top of the archway. "Perhaps if you happened to stray beneath that innocent-looking ball of greenery over there, I might just be swayed."

She shook her head, tolerant amusement shining in her eyes. She did not, however, linger under the kissing bough.

CHAPTER
EIGHT

The next morning, Pickering came into his bedchamber with none of his usual stealth, letting the door hit the wall, causing the teacup to clatter.

"Good morning, sir. Happy Christmas!"

"Pickering, you devil. Go away. It's too early."

"Not at all. You'll need ample time for a good wash and shave before dressing for church. The green coat, do you think? Sets a festive tone."

Richard pulled the bedclothes over his face and grumbled, "Never said I was going to church."

"Ah, but you did. Overheard you tell that lovely Miss Awdry."

"No. I hinted that an encounter beneath the mistletoe might sway me, but that did not happen, so I am staying in bed."

"Your hints have the subtlety of a sledgehammer. Sir, if I may be so bold—"

"Could I stop you if I tried?"

Ignoring him, Pickering went on, "A lady like Miss Awdry would be far more persuaded by gentlemanly behavior than roguish manipulation. And she would look far more kindly on a man who attended church on Christmas Day wearing his natty green coat.

Might even sit beside him, perhaps even take his arm if the way is slippery with frost."

Richard lowered the bedclothes, eyeing the old valet with begrudging admiration. "Pickering, you old Romeo . . ."

"Is that an improvement over an old devil? One is not sure. . . ."

In the end, Richard got up, washed, cleaned his teeth, and submitted to Pickering's ablutions with razor and brush. Then, dressed and oddly cheerful for such an early hour, Richard went downstairs.

After eating toast and jam and sipping tea, Richard again sneaked belowstairs. This time, he witnessed a scene very different from the grumbling of the night before. There sat Jamie, cutting out stars of dough to top the small mince tarts the cook was making. Mrs. Nettleton stood at his shoulder, clucking her approval.

"I use plenty of cinnamon, cloves, and nutmeg in my mince pies," she said. "Do you know why?"

The boy shook his head.

"They represent the gifts the magi gave to the Christ child."

"Ah."

She watched him work a moment longer. "Very good, lad. Such a good helper, you are. May I pour you some hot chocolate?"

Richard grinned and tiptoed quietly back upstairs.

At the appointed time, everyone gathered in the hall to set off for church together. The weather was mild and the way not far, so most of the party would walk. Only Lady Barbara and Lady Lillian preferred to be driven in the barouche-landau, but at least this way only one groom had to remain outdoors with the horses while the other staff could attend the service if they wished to. Most did. Many of the servants, dressed in their Sunday best, walked at a respectful distance behind the family. Pickering, Richard noticed, walked beside Mrs. Dean, the two talking like old friends.

Jamie Fleming walked near them, dressed in a fine blue coat. Richard wondered where Mrs. Dean had found it.

Seeing him looking his way, Jamie waved with a dimpled grin. Richard stood to the side, letting the others pass until Jamie caught up with him.

"Happy Christmas, Jamie."

"It is indeed, sir! And the same to you."

"Thank you. Are you enjoying yourself?"

"Don't be daft. 'Course I am!"

Richard chuckled, then caught his brother's eye.

"Timothy, Rachel, please come and meet someone." His brother and his wife stepped over. "Sir Timothy, Lady Brockwell, please allow me to introduce my new friend, Jamie Fleming."

The boy swallowed and dipped an awkward bow. "Sir. Madam. I . . . hope you don't mind me coming to your house."

"Not at all, Jamie. You are very welcome."

"Thank you."

The couple smiled at him and then walked on.

"That's your brother, sir? Seems jolly nice. Must be grand to have a brother."

"I think you're right. Though I haven't always appreciated that fact."

Reaching the churchyard, he saw Mrs. Reeves, Susanna, and her children. Susanna looked more like her old self today, dressed in a pretty frock and wearing a smile. Only the matronly cap distanced her from the Susanna he'd known. Mrs. Reeves looked cheerier too. Peter ran over to greet Mr. Murray, though they had met only once as far as Richard knew. His sister, Hannah, followed more slowly. Murray crouched low to speak to each of them, asking their favorite thing about Christmas.

The little girl shrugged shyly, but Peter energetically replied, "The Christmas pudding!"

Many other people Richard vaguely recognized clustered near the front of the church in little groups, chatting amiably. Friends and neighbors greeted one another, and many wishes of "Happy Christmas" could be heard.

Rachel's lifelong friends, Mrs. Jane Locke and Mrs. Mercy Kingsley, hurried over to greet her and to coo over young Frederick in a flowing gown with green ribbons for the special occasion.

Mrs. Kingsley's aunt, Matilda Grove, greeted the Awdrys, while village friends huddled around the Brockwell Court servants. Even Jamie found himself warmly greeted and introduced to the vicar's sons. After a moment, Richard realized that only he and his mother stood alone.

Noticing him nearby, Lady Barbara said, "Your father always loved this part. All the fawning villagers wishing him merry. Not I."

He studied her profile, stern yet vulnerable, and felt an odd mixture of emotions: distance, pity . . . love. His regal mamma, isolated by her pride. And him? What separated him from the happy throng? His long absence or disdain for home and all it entailed, including his neighbors? Remorse pricked him at the thought.

He said, "I can imagine Christmas is not a joyous time for you since losing Father."

"No, nothing is."

On impulse, he took his mother's gloved hand and found it stiff in his grasp.

"Come, Mamma. You have your children around you and are surrounded by neighbors. It's Christmas. Let's make an effort. Look, there's Matilda Grove. Shall we go and greet her?"

As if hearing her name, Matilda turned in their direction and approached with a tentative smile. "Lady Barbara, Happy Christmas. And young Richard here too! What a blessing. How long has it been?"

"Too long," his mother replied, giving his hand a squeeze.

Richard felt that squeeze through his heart.

"I quite agree," he murmured and realized he meant it.

Filing into church a short while later, their party filled the Brockwell pew and spilled into the next. He found himself seated next to Arabella Awdry. Old Pickering's prediction had been right. He'd have to give the man an extra guinea on Boxing Day.

"Slide over as far as you can," Rachel whispered down the line. "It's a full house today. Horace needs a place."

Richard, already pressed against the end of the pew, waited with sweet anticipation as Arabella sent him an apologetic look and shifted closer. The fabric of her frock brushed that of his trousers. Her shoulder touched his. After a few moments, he could feel the warmth of her body seeping into his and liked that very much indeed.

"Am I squashing you?" she whispered.

"Not at all."

She glanced at him, and then away again, whispering, "I am glad you decided to join us today."

"So am I." To himself, he added, *More than you know.*

The congregation sang, repeated the prayers still familiar from boyhood, and listened to Mr. Paley's warm, paternal voice. The vicar spoke of the miracle of Christmas and how much the Father loved everyone to send His beloved Son to earth to save all mankind.

During the sermon, Richard's gaze strayed often to his young nephew, of whom he was already quite fond. He could only imagine the all-consuming love Timothy felt for his son and knew he would give his own life to protect him. That the heavenly Father would willingly send His Son into a harsh, fallen, and dangerous world? Astounding.

After the sermon, the congregation sang "O Come, All Ye Faithful." As they did, Richard leaned nearer Arabella, longing to hear every nuance of her voice. Goodness, what a fool he was becoming. No wonder he'd avoided Ivy Hill for so long. The place did strange things to his resolve.

The fourth verse caught his attention.

> "Yea, Lord, we greet Thee, born this happy morning;
> Jesus, to Thee be glory given;
> Word of the Father, now in flesh appearing. . . ."

Word of the Father, appearing in the flesh? As a lover of words, he found that intriguing, even moving. He thought the words might be from Scripture and decided to read it later for himself, though he wasn't sure where to look.

Next they sang "Joy to the World," and then Mr. Paley dismissed them with a final blessing.

The congregants rose, more greetings were exchanged, and as they passed out the door, everyone thanked the vicar and wished him and his family every joy of the season.

As Richard walked through the churchyard, he noticed several people lined up at Craddock's just down the street. Glancing over at Rachel, he said, "I am surprised the bakery is open on Christmas Day."

Rachel nodded. "People picking up their Christmas goose. Craddock's roasts them for those without a large enough oven of their own."

"Ah. I see."

On the walk back to Brockwell Court, Pickering's second prediction came true. Arabella walked beside him.

Reaching an icy patch, she hesitated.

Richard offered his arm. "Allow me, Miss Awdry. Looks slippery."

"A slippery character indeed, miss," Pickering teased from behind. "I'd watch out for that one, if I were you."

She grinned at the old man. "Oh, I am. Never fear."

Richard enjoyed the feeling of her hand on his arm. He could get used to this.

"Do you mind?" she asked.

"Lending you my arm? Not at all. Assuming you will give it back at some point, though not too soon."

"No . . ." She looked meaningfully back at Mr. Murray and Susanna standing close to one another in friendly conversation, her little boy on his shoulders.

"Ah. Do I mind that? No, why would I?"

He looked over and found Arabella studying him through narrowed eyes.

He placed his free hand over his heart. "I am in earnest!"

She nodded and smiled gently. "Then I am glad."

When they returned to the manor, everyone put away their coats, mantles, and muffs and reconvened in the drawing room until Christmas dinner was ready, giving the servants time to finish their preparations.

Mrs. Nettleton and her staff put on quite a feast. Goose and venison with many side dishes, both savory and sweet—root vegetables, trifles, and rice pudding—followed by gingerbread and plum pudding filled with dried fruits, nutmeats, and every good thing, then basted with brandy and lit on fire.

Finally, Richard set down his table napkin and leaned back in his chair, wishing he could loosen his waistcoat. He would not eat for a week after this. Or at least until supper.

When they had finished, the servants would enjoy a well-deserved banquet of their own in the servants' hall. Richard grinned to think of Jamie's reaction to sitting down to such a feast.

After the meal, Rachel stood and said, "I realize gift-giving among adults is not expected, and that some families wait to exchange any gifts until New Year's or Twelfth Night, but since we are all together now, I have a little something for each of you."

Objections rose, and sheepish looks were exchanged around the table.

"Just something small, I promise!" their hostess soothed. Rachel, an accomplished needlewoman, had embroidered handkerchiefs for everyone, with monograms for the gentlemen and intricate flower designs for the females. She handed them round, each rolled and tied with a ribbon.

"Thank you, Rachel," Richard said dutifully along with the others, but his heart felt like a burning coal within him. He had no gifts for anyone, had not even thought of buying gifts for a single person except Justina. He would remedy that. He was glad now that his family usually waited until the New Year to give gifts. That gave him almost a week to plan.

They spent the rest of the afternoon preparing for St. Stephen's Day, or Boxing Day, on the morrow. The servants would enjoy a rare day off, so Mrs. Nettleton had prepared trays of cold meats and cheeses, breads, and salads, which the family could eat at their leisure along with leftovers from Christmas dinner.

Richard knew Mr. Paley would also be opening the church's alms box and distributing donations given in the preceding months to his poorest parishioners.

His family had already taken baskets to some villagers, but now they assembled gifts for their own servants and tenants. Those who wished to help gathered in the hall again, this time filling wooden boxes with fabric, gloves, foodstuffs, and always-welcome coins.

Miss Arabella smiled brightly through it all, clearly enjoying every minute and adding ribbons, a few coins of her own, and little notes penned with blessings for the recipients.

Richard overheard her mother say, "You see, my dear, you can do good right here in Wiltshire. No need to go off somewhere far away to do charitable things."

When Lady Lillian moved on, Richard took a step nearer to Arabella. In low, confidential tones, he asked, "Are you planning to go somewhere? I hope you don't mind, but I heard your mother mention it."

Arabella hesitated, then said, "I long to go to London, to join my aunt in her work there. Mamma tries to appease me by saying perhaps we will go to Town for a fortnight during the season and I can attend a few charity events then. But she doesn't understand. I don't want to attend one or two charity events. I want to be part of something worthwhile. Help my fellow man. Make a difference in the world."

She certainly was beautiful when she spoke so earnestly, Richard decided. Though he liked her even better when she smiled.

"I applaud you. And there is certainly no shortage of charities in the metropolis."

She sent him a wry grin. "Know from experience, do you?"

"Oh yes. I know exactly which street corners to avoid." He winked, and she laughed. Her eyes sparkled, and her pretty smile flashed.

Yes, much better. Careful, Brockwell, before you lose your head.

Later, when Richard was changing into evening attire, he asked Pickering about gifts.

"I have ideas for everyone except my mother. Any thoughts? Did Father give her presents? I don't recall."

"On occasion."

At the man's curt reply, Richard eyed his father's former valet with interest, then raised a topic he'd never before broached with him. "I'd wager he bought gifts for at least one woman in his life."

Trying to gauge his reaction as he spoke, Richard added, "You must have known about Bramble Cottage, probably long before I did."

Pickering hesitated, then replied, "Yes, I always knew."

"Did you approve?"

"Not my place to approve or disapprove. In all honesty, I thought Sir Justin was making a mistake by not marrying Georgiana Haverhill in the first place, even if his family objected."

Richard absorbed that surprising bit of news. "Did you tell him so at the time?"

"I tried. But he was not interested in my opinion. Rather like you in that regard."

"Actually, I would be interested in your views. Perhaps I would not have been in the past, but I am now."

Pickering slowly nodded. "I know you resented your father. And I don't blame you. What he did to both your mother and Miss Haverhill was wrong. But I knew him as well as anyone, and I knew he respected your mother and even came to love her over the years. You may not be aware, away at university as you were, but the last few years of his life he spent less and less time in Bramble Cottage, and more and more time in Brockwell Court. He did not abandon his responsibilities to Miss Haverhill, whose entire life he'd uprooted in bringing her to Ivy Hill, but his heart shifted and settled here at home."

Richard's own heart pounded at the thought. "If that is true, then I am sorry to have missed it."

Pickering nodded thoughtfully. "Your mother is . . . Well, she may not be the easiest woman in the world to live with, but she has many good qualities. For one, she is exceedingly loyal. In fact, that gives me an idea of a gift for her. . . ."

In the drawing room that evening, Justina struck the first chord on the pianoforte, and they again practiced the few carols they planned to sing at the almshouse that night.

Richard sat off to the side while the company practiced, as he had before. He flipped heedlessly through the *Gentleman's Magazine*, but found himself singing along.

> "While shepherds watch'd their flocks by night,
> All seated on the ground,
> The Angel of the Lord came down,
> And Glory shone all around. . . ."

Suddenly, Miss Awdry was before him, a vision in blue velvet. "You do sing, Richard. And very well too. Do say you'll join us. Your lower voice is an excellent accompaniment to Mr. Murray's tenor, while Sir Timothy . . . Well, I really want you to come with us. We need you."

Her blue eyes, wide and imploring, drew him in, and he sank into them, forgetting everything else. She'd used his Christian name. And her voice echoed in his mind. *"Richard, I want you . . . need you."*

He had no intention of agreeing, but when he opened his mouth, the treasonous words came out as if of their own volition. "Very well. If you insist."

"I do!" She beamed at him. "Thank you. Everyone, Richard has agreed to come with us!"

Had he? He blinked, as though coming out of a trance. Yes, he supposed he had.

"Huzzah!" Justina exclaimed, and came over and kissed his cheek.

He smiled at her but could not help wishing another female had kissed him.

They all bundled up in their warmest pelisses, coats, and capes and carried candle lamps to illuminate their sheet music. Jamie Fleming, doing a favor for Mrs. Nettleton, brought up a basket filled with small mince tarts topped with a star-shaped pastry, and almond biscuits from the Brockwell Court kitchens. Rachel thanked him.

Richard asked, "Would you like to come along, Jamie?"

"Yes, sir. I would. Just let me make sure it is all right with Mrs. Dean and Mrs. Nettleton."

A short while later, they all strolled down the drive and up the High Street together, talking softly amongst themselves as they went. Justina and Nicholas shared one lamp, as did Horace and Penelope, Rachel and Sir Timothy, Richard and Arabella, and Murray and Jamie, who seemed happy to be in their company.

Richard looked down at Arabella. "Are you sure you're not too cold? We could have taken the curricle."

"I am perfectly well, but thank you for your concern."

He *was* concerned about her well-being, he realized. *Dash it all.*

She smiled, adding, "It was kind of you to invite Jamie."

He nodded, then winked. "Let's just hope he sings better than Timothy."

When they reached the almshouse, the carolers clustered near the door and, at Rachel's signal, began singing, "God Rest Ye Merry, Gentlemen."

The front door opened, and the matron, Mrs. Mennell, appeared. "Please come in!" she beckoned. "Not everyone is able to come to the door."

So the little troupe filed inside, squeezing into the entryway. In the small parlour sat the same elderly women and single man they'd seen on their last visit, lap rugs over their legs, and some with teacups in their gnarled fingers. They all turned eager eyes on the inexperienced but willing carolers, who next sang "The First Noel."

As the last note fell away, the small crowd clapped appreciatively and Richard noticed tears in more than one pair of weary eyes. Something in his chest cracked, then loosened, and a tendril of joy sprouted in his heart.

One of the women grasped Arabella's hand. "You sing like an angel, child. You may come and sing for me anytime you like."

Arabella smiled at her. "Thank you, Mrs. Russell. I shall."

Their effusive gratitude for the modest offering both touched and humbled Richard.

While Rachel handed round the mince tarts and almond biscuits, Richard stepped into the parlour and shook the old man's hand.

"We gents have to stick together," he said with a grin. "What's it like being the only rooster in a henhouse?"

"A trial, in all truth." The old man winked. "Tiring to fight them off night and day."

Richard chuckled at the man's joke.

They stayed to visit awhile longer, then walked home, singing softly as they went.

Richard reached over and squeezed Arabella's hand. "Thank you for making me go, Miss Awdry. I am surprised—I actually enjoyed that."

Her eyes shone by lamplight. "I am glad."

They returned to the house, and after shedding their coats, sat before a blazing fire, the massive Yule log and hazel branches providing cheery light and welcome warmth. The footman brought in hot spiced cider and punch, which further warmed the company. He soon returned with trays of Christmas fare: widgeon, black butter, sandwiches, mince tarts, and glasses of syllabub.

Justina sat beside Richard and briefly rested her head against his shoulder. "Thank you for coming home, Richard. It was the best gift you could have given us."

Laying his hand over his sister's, Richard stared into the fire and felt the smoke burn his eyes.

CHAPTER

NINE

When Richard went downstairs the next morning, he nearly collided with Susanna in the passage.

"Ah, Susanna. Um . . . welcome." If he felt awkward, how must she be feeling?

She wore a long bibbed apron over a plain grey frock. A white mobcap covered most of her dark hair.

"Mr. Brockwell." She bobbed a slight curtsy, avoiding his eyes and passing by—the actions of servant.

It stung him.

"Susanna . . ." he called after her, his tone carrying his hurt.

She paused, her back to him. He saw her shoulders rise and fall with a deep breath, then she turned and resolutely strode back to him.

Facing him squarely, she said, "I am here as a servant, not as a friend. At least I hope so, for if I am only here because of our past . . . friendship, then I shall give notice directly."

He winced. "There's no need for that. Lady Brockwell sincerely wished to engage a nurserymaid. Upon my honor. Such as it is."

"Precisely." Her eyes glimmered with sadness, then she released a heavy sigh. "You must treat me as any other servant in your family's employ. Do you understand? This is only my first day, so I will speak plainly, and then we need not speak again."

"That seems harsh."

"Do you speak to the other servants? To Nurse Pocket?"

He shuddered. "Never, if I can help it."

"There, you see?"

"That's only because she was my own nurse and frightened me to death as a child. Still does. But I speak to Andrew and Carville and Mrs. Dean and the rest. And Pickering and I talk all the time. Him mostly complaining, but still . . ."

"But I doubt you chat up the housemaids. At least I hope you don't."

He stepped closer and lowered his voice. "I know you are angry with me, Susanna, and I don't blame you. Can we not at least treat one another civilly when you're here?"

She hesitated. "Civilly, but no more."

Again her words, her distrust, stung him.

At the sound of a door closing down the passage, Susanna took a long step back. She bobbed another curtsy, her expression falling back into servile blandness.

"Very good, Mr. Brockwell. Will that be all?"

He glanced over his shoulder, expecting Rachel or perhaps Mrs. Dean. Instead, Arabella stood there, looking from him to Susanna and back again, her face darkened by shadows . . . and suspicion.

Since it was Boxing Day, Horace and Penelope rode off together to join a fox hunt being held at a friend's estate in nearby Hampshire.

Sir Timothy and Rachel were busy giving gifts to their servants and tenants, and receiving tokens and words of gratitude in return. Arabella had asked if there was anything she could do to help, and they'd invited her to accompany them.

Justina and Mr. Ashford went to Thornvale to spend time with his mother. Mrs. Ashford had invited an old school friend to stay for Christmas, or she would have come to the house party as well. From what he'd heard about the unkind woman, Richard could only be thankful for small mercies.

Richard went to Murray's room but found him busy editing. Murray reminded him that he should be busy writing his next piece. Richard did work on revising his second novel for an hour but knew he could not put off much longer the task he least wanted to do—delivering Jamie back to Wishford.

Taking Wally with them, Richard drove Jamie back to Wishford that afternoon, to make sure he returned well before Mr. Knock.

They left the horses and carriage in the livery and walked slowly to the shop, Jamie quiet but resigned. Richard, hamper in hand, was not eager to leave the boy there but knew he must. There were, however, two things he hoped would improve the lad's living conditions: a basket of provisions and a plan.

At the shop door, Jamie turned to him and held out his hand. "Thank you, Mr. Brockwell. It was the best Christmas I ever had."

Richard pressed the chilled fingers. "You are very welcome, Jamie." He handed over the hamper. "From Mrs. Nettleton. Keep it in the garret with you. It's for you alone."

"Thank you, sir. You are all so kind."

Jamie waved in farewell and dug out the key.

"May I come in for a few minutes?" Richard asked.

The boy shrugged. "That's all right, sir. I don't mind being alone. It's not even dark yet."

"This is not a social call. Wally and I have a job to do."

The boy bunched up his face. "What do you mean?"

"Wally wants to investigate the garret. He's heard rumors of a large rodent in residence."

Jamie's eyes widened. "Really? But it's almost as big as he is!"

"Do you want the menace gone or don't you?"

Jamie unlocked the door and opened it. "I do, yes. If you think he is equal to it."

"You wound us both. Of course he is equal to it. It is what terriers like him have been bred for."

Jamie looked at the dandy little dog skeptically. Perhaps Richard ought to have foregone the bow atop his head.

"He may not look the warrior, but he is one."

As if to refute Richard's claim, the dog lay down and began licking a cobweb from his paw.

"Well, he may have grown a bit fat and spoiled in recent days. But when he first came to live with me, he cleared the cellar of several mice and earned my housekeeper's love forever."

"I'd hate to put him at risk, sir. A rat is lots bigger and meaner than a mouse. If anything were to happen to your dog because of me, I'd never forgive myself."

You, dear boy, are far more important than any animal, Richard thought. But he said, "Wally here would gladly lay down his life for you. Never doubt it. But it won't come to that. Now, enough naysaying. You don't want to steal his confidence. Lead on."

"Very well, sir."

Jamie led him up one pair of stairs, then up a set of steep narrow steps more like a ladder than a staircase.

Richard picked up Wally and carried him, using his free hand to steady himself on the rungs above.

When they reached the garret, Richard saw the boy had not exaggerated in his description. The roof was in far worse state than Honeycroft's. The smell of mold and damp permeated the air. A small pallet bed without pillow—blanket neatly folded—had been pushed to one side, as far from the gaping hole as possible.

Richard looked around the room's dingy confines. "Where is he?"

"I don't know, sir. I don't usually see him till dark."

Wally began wriggling in Richard's arms. He hoped the dog didn't have to relieve himself, now of all times. But when he set him down, the animal quickly began to sniff the floor, posture alert, on the scent of something. He dodged into a dim corner, and with a sudden lunge and violent shake, he wrenched the neck of something lurking there before Richard had even laid eyes on the thing.

Wally gave it a final sniff and then, satisfied the rodent was dead, happily trotted around the room, then laid down again, this time at Jamie's feet.

Richard tentatively approached the still form.

It was perhaps not the stuff of legends. Jamie may have exaggerated its size slightly—for fear and darkness and chewed bedclothes will do that. But the thing was certainly bigger than a mouse, bigger than several mice. Imagine trying to sleep just waiting for that thing to come nibbling at you? Richard shivered.

Then he knelt before Wally to give him all the honor due him, stroking his fur and promising a steak from Mrs. Nettleton's larder. When she wasn't looking, of course.

As Jamie approached, his eyes widened with awe. "He did it! I can't believe he did it. Just like that! You were right, Mr. Brockwell. He is small but ever so brave."

Richard's gaze remained on the child who had already endured so much, thinking, *Yes, he is.*

Back at Brockwell Court, Richard sat down and wrote an impassioned article about the plight of apprentices, hoping Murray would want to print it in his magazine. He had already sent a scathing letter to the charity's board of governors, who had sentenced Jamie to his fate. But who knew if or when he would receive a reply. Hopefully the article would prove more effective.

Later that afternoon, he let Wally outside, and as the dog bounded off to water a topiary, Richard wrapped his arms around himself against the chill. *Brrr.* The day had turned biting and crisp and smelled of snow. He wondered how cold it must be inside Honeycroft on such a day, and the worst of winter was yet to come.

When the family carriage returned to Brockwell Court, Richard laid aside his pride and went to ask his brother for help with Honeycroft. He found Timothy in his office—their father's old office, where Sir Justin had once performed the magisterial duties that his eldest son now carried out. He knocked and gingerly let himself in. Oh, the unpleasant memories of reprimands and lectures that still echoed within its walls.

Timothy sat bent over paper and ink and held up an index finger. "Give me one minute, please."

While he waited, Richard looked at his older brother and noticed his dark side-whiskers were threaded with silver, though he was only two and thirty. Their father had also greyed early. Richard's own hair was still as dark as ever.

His brother blotted the paper and looked up. "Thank you for waiting. What is it, Richard?"

Richard sat down but hesitated. His brother interlaced his fingers over his appointment diary. "Is something wrong?"

"Yes, unfortunately. I hate to ask, but I need help."

Timothy's eyes flattened. "Richard, I hope you are not going to ask for money. We have talked about this before."

"Not for me. You know Susanna, our new nurserymaid?"

"Oh no. Tell me you have not wronged her already."

"Thunder and turf!" Richard leaned back heavily in his chair, stunned. "You really do think me a reprobate!"

"Well . . . Rachel told me you knew her in the past, and that you wanted to help her, so—"

Richard raised a hand to stop him. "I have treated her with the utmost propriety since my arrival, I promise you. Yes, I disappointed her in the past. Years ago. But that is not what this about. Well, I suppose it is, in a way. I want to make recompense. She and her brother and parents were very good to me when I was young. And I'd like to return the favor now."

Timothy frowned. "I knew you and Seth were friends, but I did not realize you spent that much time with the family."

"I did. You know I did not get on with Father. Barely better with Mamma. Mr. and Mrs. Reeves were there for me when I needed them. They were like a second family to me."

Timothy's expression darkened. "I am sorry to hear your first family was insufficient to the purpose."

Richard raised a palm. "I am not here to lay blame or complain. Thing is, Honeycroft has fallen into disrepair since Mr. Reeves died. It needs some work to shore it up for winter. I went to see the Kingsleys, but they haven't the time, and even if they did, the estimate is beyond my means."

"And no wonder, as you have lived beyond your means for years."

For a moment the two brothers glared at one another, then Timothy sat back, changing tack. "By the way, it's no secret Mamma hopes to instigate a match between you and Miss Awdry, but if you think I am in on it, you are mistaken. I have cautioned her against it, and I caution you as well."

Richard frowned. "You don't think I am good enough for her?"

"I didn't say that. But as it is, what sort of life could you offer her?"

"I am not offering her anything. I doubt she would have me at any rate. Too clever by far. And you know I am a determined bachelor."

"Not as determined as you once were. I have seen how you look at her." Timothy sighed and ran a hand through his hair. "I had planned to wait to raise the topic until later, but since we are discussing money, I have to tell you that after reviewing the estate finances, I agree with Mamma that it simply does not make fiscal sense to keep the London house open year-round simply so you can continue your separate life there."

"What?"

"You are one person. And you have a valet and cook-housekeeper at your disposal, not to mention kitchen and housemaids."

"It is a far smaller staff than we once had."

"Yes, when we all spent time in London. These days we rarely go for the season, let alone any other time. We have an excellent house here with sufficient staff and more than enough room for us all. You are nearly thirty years old, with no independent means.

It isn't as though you have a situation or responsibilities to keep you in Town and justify the expense."

"I have my friends. My . . . club." Richard swallowed the phrase "my work."

"That is hardly going to strengthen your case. At all events, Mamma and I are in agreement. We plan to sell the townhouse in the new year."

Richard sputtered, "But . . . but that is my home!"

"*This* is your home. Why Father ever consented to letting you live in London and footing the bill, I'll never know."

"No, you don't know. But he had his reasons for wanting me gone, and I had mine for wanting to be anywhere but here. That has not changed."

"But it has. Father is gone. He may have verbally offered you use of the London property, but there were no bequests in his will. We need to think of the future. I am managing the estate now, and I have to do what is best for the entire family, not just one member."

"You do like to lord that over me, don't you? The eldest son and heir, Sir Timothy, trying so hard to fill Sir Justin's shoes. I hope you don't emulate all his ways."

Timothy stared hard at Richard. "What do you mean?"

Richard hesitated. "Never mind." He huffed a sigh. "Look, I did not come in here to argue with you or to ask for money for myself. I came to ask for help with Honeycroft. For all his faults, Father would have helped."

A muscle in Timothy's clenched jaw pulsed, and his nostrils flared. Then he sighed. "You're right, he would have. Very well. Let's go take another look at the place together. Our farm manager has some building experience, and we have plenty of lumber and slate in the outbuildings. Perhaps between us, we can patch up the place."

Mrs. Reeves answered the door, shawl around her shoulders, a look of unease on her face. "Richard, what are you doing back so soon? Is Susanna all right?"

"Yes, perfectly well." He turned to include his brother. "Have you met my brother, Sir Timothy?"

She nodded. "A pleasure to see you again, sir. I trust your wee boy fares well?"

"Yes, and he adores your daughter already."

"Good. Well, come in, come in. What can I do for you gentlemen?"

Standing inside the main room, Richard saw his brother's gaze shift from the boarded-up window to the buckets on the floor under a suspicious dark stain on the ceiling.

"Actually, we are here to see what we might do about your leaking roof and broken window before Old Man Winter gives us his worst."

She grimaced. "I did have the Kingsley brothers out to give me an estimate, but I . . . decided to put it off. It's not so bad."

As if to argue the point, another plop of soaking wet plaster fell from the ceiling and splashed into the bucket.

"Mrs. Reeves, forgive me," Richard said, "but it is like an icehouse in here, even with the fire burning."

She winced in apology. "I know. I feel bad for the children, though they don't seem to mind the cold, busy running about and playing as they are. But I . . ." She pulled her shawl more closely about herself, and Richard noticed she wore gloves indoors. "I could not repay you."

Richard smiled. "Of course you can. You can repay us with a ready supply of Reeves's famous honey in the years to come."

She worried her lip. "I am afraid our bees are not doing well either. The hives are not producing what they once did."

"We'll sort that too. Won't we, Timothy?"

His brother looked less certain. "Oh, em, yes. If we can."

She shook her head. "It's too much to ask."

Richard rested a hand on her shoulder. "Not a bit of it. It is the least I can do. It won't begin to repay you for all the meals you fed me as a boy, nor all the pleasant hours I spent in your company."

"You *did* have quite an appetite," Mrs. Reeves allowed.

Richard smiled at her teasing, and his heart warmed to see the old twinkle sparking to life in her eyes.

Later that afternoon they returned with the farm manager, Mr. Grayson, as well as their groundsman. The men inspected the roof and window and discovered broken gutters were contributing to the leaking windows.

They decided on a plan of action and agreed to start early the next morning.

Pickering tentatively woke Richard early the next morning as he'd requested, but the old man was clearly surprised when Richard thanked him and all but sprang from bed and began washing.

"Your best coat today, sir?" the valet asked.

"No, my worst. I am going to be a workman today. Help me dress the part."

Pickering coughed. "I believe you are the first man in the kingdom to utter those words."

Richard chuckled. "Good point. I shall dress myself. But may I leave Wally with you? I don't want him underfoot."

"Very well."

Richard and Murray wolfed down a quick breakfast and hastened to Honeycroft. Reaching it before anyone else, they were ready to help unload supplies when the Brockwell Court wagon rumbled up the lane, heavy with lumber, slate, and tools. Mr. Jones, the groundsman, drove, and beside him on the bench sat Mr. Grayson, the farm manager.

"Morning, Jones. Grayson."

"Morning, sir."

"We're here to help," Richard said, hands on hips. "Put us to work."

The manager's mouth fell open. "You, sir?"

"Sarcasm does not become you. Yes, me."

"Very well. Let's unload the lumber first."

As the morning progressed, more people joined them. As was often the case in a small village like Ivy Hill, word of the project spread quickly. Perhaps due to the Christmas season, Mrs. Reeves's kindness, or the fact that the village's leading family was involved, several came to help.

Joseph Kingsley, who had married Rachel's friend Mercy Grove, arrived, armed with his tool bag. He said he was sorry his brother had sent him away empty-handed. It was true they were busy, but he would offer his own time and expertise to help for the day.

Richard thanked him.

Later, the slater and stout Mr. Broadbent, the plumber, also joined them. While Murray held the ladder, Mr. Broadbent repaired the gutters, and the slater advised and assisted those repairing the roof. Richard kept busy carrying slate tiles from the wagon. Quickly growing warm from his exertions, he discarded his outer coat, working in his waistcoat and shirtsleeves.

Mr. Jones, as groundsman, had some experience with beehives and did what he could to set them to rights. He said, "However well made the skep may be, it is important to protect them from rain and snow. A dry hive in winter is essential." To cover the hives. he made new conical straw hackles, which would shed water like the thatch of a barn.

Mrs. Reeves brought out honey-sweetened tea for the men, lamenting that she had not more refreshment to offer the volunteers. As if in answer to her prayers, women from the Ladies Tea and Knitting Society arrived with baskets of food for the workmen— freshly made rolls, butter and cheese from the dairy, along with pies and sweets left over from Christmas dinners all across the village. They spread several boards across two sawhorses to create a makeshift banquet table.

The Brockwell Court barouche-landau arrived, top up against the cold breeze. Richard saw Timothy inside, holding a bundled-up Frederick, Rachel next to him, and beside her, Susanna herself.

Stepping down first, Timothy held his son with one arm and offered his free hand to help the ladies descend.

Rachel looked at the spread of food and lifted her basket with a chuckle. "And here I thought you might be going hungry." With good humor and warmth, she greeted her friends from the Ladies Tea and Knitting Society and added food from the Brockwell larder to the other offerings.

Susanna looked around at the workmen and assembled neighbors with an expression of amazement. For a moment her gaze locked with Richard's, and then she walked nearer and said, "Thank you."

He shrugged. "I have done precious little indeed. You know I am good for nothing."

She slowly shook her head, eyes warm. "That is not true. It wasn't true when I said it, and it is not true now."

He nodded gravely. "I hope you are right."

Susanna turned to include David Murray in their conversation. "My thanks to you as well, Mr. Murray. I'm guessing you did not count on being put to work here. I hope this doesn't spoil your Christmas."

"Not at all. In fact, I am enjoying myself immensely."

Susanna smiled at Murray. "I am glad to hear it."

Richard had almost forgotten how beautiful she could be when she smiled.

While the Brockwell brothers, Rachel, and Mr. Murray were busy at Honeycroft, Arabella and Justina went to the Fairmont School in the Awdrys' coach. In her reticule, Arabella carried an embroidered handkerchief Rachel had made for Mercy but had not had a chance to deliver with all the busyness of the house party.

With a glance at her companion, Arabella said, "Thank you for coming with me, Justina."

"My pleasure. I look forward to seeing the school myself."

Justina had brought a leather portfolio with sheet music inside, so she might accompany Arabella on the school's pianoforte. Or if the old harp was in no fit condition, Arabella would sing while Justina played, and perhaps lead the children in a few songs.

Reaching the former Fairmont House, the two ladies alighted and crossed the half-circle drive to the front entrance.

Mercy Kingsley met them at the door.

"Welcome, Miss Awdry. Justina. How good of you to come."

Justina said, "I thought I might accompany Arabella on your pianoforte, if you don't mind."

"Not at all. Mrs. Klein keeps it in tune for us, though I have no idea in what state you will find the harp. It looks all right, but I know nothing about the instrument."

Arabella smiled. "Let me take a look—and a listen."

From the vestibule, Mercy led them through a reception room and into a large common room, with game tables, shelves of books and games, and clusters of chairs and sofas. A harp had been positioned near the pianoforte.

"Oh, it's beautiful . . ." Arabella breathed, running her hand over the ornate carving of the single action pedal harp. "Must be a hundred years old."

Arabella sat down on the stool Mercy had provided and plucked experimentally at the strings. "It sounds better than I imagined after being stored all these years." She began playing a piece by Mozart, who had written such beautiful harp music.

As if her playing were a siren call, children began streaming into the room, coming from all directions, drawn by the sound. Soon a dozen children of varying ages were gathered around the instruments, sitting on the sofas, chairs, or floor.

"We have more students, but some have gone home for Christmas," Mercy explained.

Miss Matilda Grove joined them along with a darker-skinned man she introduced as Mr. Basu.

Justina played the pianoforte, and Arabella the beautiful old harp. It wasn't perfect—the instrument or the performance—but the children were enthralled and clapped profusely when they finished. Arabella had never had such an appreciative audience. Next they performed another piece, one by Dussek.

Afterward, they decided to play a few Christmas songs, and the children sang along.

They ended their little concert with "Adeste Fideles."

"Beautiful!" Miss Matilda enthused. "Absolutely beautiful."

A maid brought out tea, warm milk, and shortbread for everyone to enjoy. Then the older children were allowed to pluck the harp under Arabella's guidance.

While Justina read the children a story, Arabella slipped back into the vestibule, where she'd left her pelisse and reticule, to retrieve Rachel's small gift. But at the doorway, she drew up short. For there stood Mercy with her tall husband, apparently just returning home, tool bag in hand. His arm was wrapped around his wife, while she lifted both hands to his face and rose on tiptoes to meet his passionate kiss.

Good heavens.

"I missed you, my love," he whispered, eyes for no one but his wife.

"And I you."

Arabella quietly retreated. The handkerchief would wait. Rejoining the others, she thought, *If I could have a loving marriage like that . . . I just might change my mind about avoiding it.*

Richard and Murray returned to Brockwell Court weary but content and went to their separate rooms to wash and change into evening dress. At the designated hour, all the scattered houseguests assembled for a dinner. Penelope and Horace were full of tales of their successful hunt. Nicholas and Justina smiled at one another almost constantly, while Mamma tsked and shook her head. And Arabella and Justina talked with enthusiasm of their time at the Fairmont School.

At one point, Arabella leaned closer to Richard and asked, "You're quiet tonight. Thinking of Jamie back in Wishford?"

He nodded. "Yes, among other things." But he did not elaborate.

After the meal, most everyone gathered in the drawing room as usual. His mother and Lady Lillian, however, excused themselves and retired early.

While they waited for tea and coffee to be served, Justina suggested a parlour game. "Unless you had something else planned, Rachel?"

Rachel shook her head. "Not at all. Which game did you have in mind?"

"Perhaps, move all?" Justina looked at the others. "Does everyone know that one?"

Murray said sheepishly, "I don't, I'm afraid. But I will happily watch."

"No, you must join in, Mr. Murray. I insist."

Timothy leaned back on the sofa. "I'll sit this one out, if you don't mind."

"Me too," Rachel added, taking her place beside him.

"Because you are old married people now?" Justina teased. "Oh, very well."

Justina directed the men to position six chairs in a circle, spaced as far apart as possible.

When everyone except herself was seated, she began, "Now, when I say 'Move all,' everyone must get up and find a new seat, including me. Whoever is left without a chair must pay a forfeit and become the next caller."

Richard crossed a casual ankle over his leg. "And what will the forfeit be?"

Justina waggled her eyebrows. "That is for the caller to decide."

Murray shifted uneasily, murmuring, "As long as I am not required to dance . . . or recite from *Debrett's Peerage*."

"Or sew," Penelope added with a shudder.

Justina went on to say, "If you don't change chairs, you will pay two forfeits. Any questions?"

She glanced around the circle. Richard winked at her.

Then Justina raised her hand. "Ready? Move all!"

Everyone rose. Penelope darted to the seat to her left, and Arabella seized her vacated chair. Horace dashed across the room, nearly colliding with Nicholas. He veered toward Arabella's chair, but Richard beat him to it.

Looking around uncertainly, Justina hurried toward an empty chair across the circle, but Nicholas and David Murray were several steps ahead of her. Murray claimed the chair with a triumphant grin. Justina and Nicholas dashed for the last remaining chair. Spinning around to sit on it, they both landed on half a seat. Nicholas smiled at her, then stood and threw up his hands up in mock despair.

Justina slid fully onto the chair with a laugh, beaming up at him.

Nicholas grinned back. "And now I must pay a forfeit. What shall it be, Miss Brockwell?"

Justina tapped a finger to her chin. "Why don't you recite something?"

Penelope made a face. "Or he could just hop on one leg and be done with it."

"What fun would that be?" Richard said. "Go on, man."

Nicholas's brow furrowed as he looked up in thought, hands folded behind his back. Then he spoke with surprising, steady conviction, "'This above all: to thine own self be true. And it must follow, as the night the day, Thou canst not then be false to any man.'"

After a pause, Nicholas bowed. Everyone clapped.

"Shakespeare," said Richard. "Excellent choice."

"Yes, from *Hamlet*," added Arabella. "Well done, Mr. Ashford."

"Thank you."

Then Nicholas acted as caller for the second round, announcing, "Move all."

Again everyone rose. Arabella scrambled into Justina's vacated seat. With a squeal, Justina plopped down into her brother's empty chair just before Penelope reached it. Penelope spun toward a chair on her left as Horace Bingley launched himself toward the same prize. Penelope landed first, and Horace all but landed on her lap, instantly reddening.

"Forgive me!" He shot up, and started toward the remaining chair, but Richard reached it before him. That left Horace wheeling in the center of the room, until finally he chuckled. "A forfeit it is, then."

Nicholas considered, then said, "Tell us something about yourself, Mr. Bingley."

"Something unrelated to sport, please," advised Justina. "You have already told us how many pheasants you shot last season."

"I personally found it rather interesting," Penelope assured him.

Horace seemed at a loss, but then his face brightened. "Very well. I don't know how interesting it is, but as a lad, I once rescued an injured crow. It became quite tame. But after it healed, it escaped my room, flew downstairs, and landed on the head of one of our dinner guests."

The others chuckled appreciatively.

"Mamma forbade me to keep it in the house after that. But it still came and perched on my window ledge almost every day for the rest of that summer."

Penelope studied his face, admiration in her eyes. "Impressive."

Horace shrugged and met her gaze with a smile.

On the next round, David Murray was the odd man out.

"For your forfeit," Horace said. "Tell us about your favorite Christmas ever."

Murray nodded, perfectly serious, then looked from person to person. "This one."

"Come now, that's going it a bit brown," Horace protested.

Rachel joined in, adding, "That is kind of you, but you needn't say so."

"Not at all. It's true. My childhood was not a happy one, and I have been on my own for years. I'd almost forgot what it's like to be a part of a family, and a loving family no less."

A moment of thoughtful, even awkward, silence followed. Then Timothy spoke up, "Well said, Mr. Murray. We are blessed indeed to be together this Christmas, and we are thankful each and every one of you has joined us."

Richard said, "Hear, hear."

And he found he actually meant it.

They began another round of the game. Near its end, Arabella hurried toward a chair at the same time Richard approached. With a gallant wave and bow, he gestured for her to take it. Turning, he only then realized no other chairs remained.

He gave an exaggerated sigh. "That will teach me to be chivalrous." He turned to Mr. Murray with a smirk. "What shall my forfeit be?"

Arabella hoped his friend would require something challenging. Mr. Murray tilted his head up. "Let me think . . ."

At that moment, the door opened and the pretty woman in a plain grey dress and white apron came in with little Frederick in arms.

Rachel said, "Ah, our new nurserymaid. You are here late, Susanna. Everything all right?"

"Master Frederick is struggling to fall asleep. I thought a goodnight kiss from his mamma might help."

"Good idea."

Rachel and Timothy walked over to cuddle the child, but Arabella's eyes remained on the woman. The same woman they had passed when out walking. And whom she had seen talking with Richard in clandestine fashion that very morning, the two whispering with their heads near like old friends . . . or lovers.

Mr. Murray finally announced his forfeit. "You must answer this question: If you could go back in time and change one thing about your past, what would it be?"

Mr. Brockwell's eyes dimmed, and his confident smirk faded, but whether from Murray's question or the woman's entrance, Arabella did not know. Either way, Richard looked uncharacteristically nervous, clasping and unclasping his hands, a self-conscious smile flickering, then falling away. She began to feel sorry for him.

"Change only one thing about my past?" he said. "But there are so many to choose from."

He gave a bleak little chuckle, his expression serious as he seemed to consider the question. Around him the others waited, his friend and sister with interest, Horace and Penelope clearly feeling ill at ease as the moment lengthened.

Arabella was just about to suggest an alternate forfeit, when Richard quietly replied, "I would not disappoint someone I care about."

Was it her imagination or did he glance at Susanna as he said it?

"What does that mean?" Justina asked, eyes sparking with interest. "How mysterious!"

As if suddenly recalled to his surroundings, Richard straightened and waved a dismissive hand. "Nothing. Pure foolishness. Too much wine." Though Arabella had not seen him sip one drop.

Thanking the nurserymaid for staying late, Rachel urged her to go on home, saying she would take Frederick up to bed in a few minutes. The woman bobbed a curtsy and departed.

They played one final round of the game, and this time Arabella was left without a chair.

Richard rallied, standing and rubbing his hands together. "Ah, what an opportunity. What forfeit shall I require of the lovely Miss Arabella?" He tapped his lower lip in thought.

"Careful, Richard," Sir Timothy warned under his breath.

Richard's eyes glinted with mischief. "For your forfeit, you shall kiss the most handsome man in the room."

Justina gasped, though humor shone in her expression. "You are too bad, Richard."

"Let us keep things civilized, please," Rachel said. "No one shall kiss anyone."

"Well now, let us not get carried away . . ." Timothy objected glibly, with a grin for his wife.

Rachel amended, "That is, no one is required to kiss anyone they don't wish to." She winked at her husband. "Unless they are under the mistletoe."

Arabella squared her shoulders and announced, "I don't mind. In fact, there is little I would enjoy more."

Around the room, stunned looks were exchanged.

She strode toward Richard, and he stood straighter, posture tense, eyes alert, expression uncertain. But she walked right past him, crossing the room to where Rachel held Frederick, and kissed the little boy on the forehead.

"There, I've kissed the most handsome male in the room."

Rachel nodded, "I quite agree."

The others chuckled. Everyone except Richard. He crossed his arms, feigning pique. "That's not fair."

"Point and game to Arabella," Mr. Murray said, giving Richard a good-natured slap on the back. "I'd say you've met your match, Brockwell."

Arabella took Frederick in her arms and pretended not to hear.

CHAPTER

ELEVEN

As Richard prepared for bed that night, Murray's words echoed through his mind, *"I'd say you've met your match, Brockwell."* Richard was beginning to agree. He could still see Arabella standing there, cuddling his nephew. The image of the beautiful woman displaying love and affection did strange things to his heart.

They continued the repair work on Saturday, but the next day being Sunday, they rested from their labors. Richard had never been so tired or sore. He slept in, ignoring Pickering's proddings that he attend church again. Instead, after eating eggs and toast, he took some willow bark tea for his aches and pains and went back to bed.

Pickering muttered under his breath, "Two steps forward and one step back."

Richard retorted, "Rome wasn't built in a day, Pickering."

Later that afternoon, he took Wally outside for his begged-for walk. Of old habit, Richard's feet took him to Honeycroft. The children were playing in the front garden when he arrived. He left Wally outside with them.

At the door, Mrs. Reeves met him with a smile. "Oh, my boy. So good to see you again."

"You are not tired of seeing me yet?"

"Not at all. You are always welcome."

He noticed she still wore a shawl indoors but this time no gloves. "How are you feeling?" he asked.

"Much better, thank you. The cottage is warmer already! Come in and sit down, and I'll make us the last of the tea. I've been saving it for you."

Why was she so happy to see him? Why would she celebrate his return? The guilt of it sat heavy on his chest. Richard said, "You are too good to me, Mrs. Reeves. You should not be so kind. Not when I abandoned you all."

"Oh, Richard. That is all in the past. All forgiven." She patted his hand. "And not because you are helping to fix up this old place. I forgave you long ago."

He shook his head. "You don't know what I've done, or you would not say so."

Her expression sobered. "I do know. Susanna confided everything years ago. She may not have forgiven you, but I have."

"Don't. I hurt and disappointed Susanna, and disappointed you afterward. I don't deserve forgiveness."

Her eyes snapped. "You're right. You don't deserve it. Love and forgiveness are not something you earn. They are gifts. My, my, have I neglected your education so terribly? My dear boy, none of us *deserves* forgiveness. None of us can do enough good deeds to atone for our own failings. If we could, God would not have had to send the Son He loved into the world to die for us. But He did, because He loves us."

Richard thought once more of the words the vicar had spoken on Christmas. That the heavenly Father would willingly send His precious Son into a world He knew would crucify Him? Richard felt astounded all over again and not a little incredulous.

"Do you really believe that?" he asked her.

"I do, yes, utterly and completely. Surely you know me well enough not to be surprised by that! Why do you think we invited you in all those years ago? Because we are so good, or you are so charming?" She shook her head, a soft smile on her lined face. "No, it was because Mr. Reeves and I felt God nudge our hearts, whisper to us that we could be of some help to you. At first, we didn't realize you were from the manor. We assumed you were some village boy. Only God would know the younger son of a baronet needed us."

Richard managed a bleak chuckle.

She squeezed his hand. "And perhaps it is time to forgive Sir Justin. For your own sake. Forgive and be forgiven, as the Scriptures say. No, he was not a perfect man. He did wrong. But so have you."

Richard nodded. "I will try."

"Try? What is 'try'?" Her eyes snapped again. "Every day God gives us, we must do our best to trust and obey. We fail, but we do the same the next day, clinging to His promises and strength to help us. If that is your definition of *try*, then I am satisfied. But if it is lip service to something that's difficult so you will give up after a few attempts, well then, I am not."

"Good night, you are being tough on me today."

She sighed. "I know. But life is short, and there is no sense in wasting words. I care for you too much to not tell you the truth."

Mrs. Reeves looked off into the distance. Into the past. "I wish I'd told Seth more of what was on my heart while I could. I hope when he died, it was with a prayer on his lips."

Tears shone in her weary eyes, and Richard felt tears prick his own eyes in reply.

"I have no doubt of it. Seth even wrote to me once, urging me to seek God's help and forgiveness as you taught us. So I am sure he was ready to meet his Maker, thanks to you."

She shook her head. "Not thanks to me. Thanks to our Savior." She looked back at him, gaze resolute. "You remember that, my boy."

"I will tr—" He stopped, and started again. "I will."

They completed the repairs on Monday. Richard saw the project through to the last, even helping to load lumber scraps, broken slates, and tools back into the wagon.

Mrs. Snyder, the laundress, had come and helped Mrs. Reeves take down the curtains that had been stained by the foul leaking water. Together the two women hung up the freshly laundered curtains, and the room looked brighter and more inviting than before. Mrs. Reeves did too.

Finally all was finished. Mrs. Reeves thanked everyone profusely and kissed Richard's cheek. "Thank you, lad. Mr. Reeves would have been so proud of you. Your own father as well."

He ducked his head. "Thank you, Mrs. Reeves." He hoped it was true.

As they walked home together, Timothy said, "She's right, you know. Father was not perfect, but he would have been proud of you. I know I am."

Richard's heart pounded, and his throat tightened. He wanted to thank his brother but could not speak for the lump in his throat.

When he returned to Brockwell Court, weary but content, Richard found himself filled with an unusual emotion—the satisfaction of a job well done.

A letter was waiting for him on the hall table—forwarded from London. Looking at the postal markings, he saw that it had been posted to the townhouse just after he'd left London. His housekeeper must have forwarded it on to him before closing up the house for a few days at Christmas.

He opened it and saw it was from the third publisher he'd approached about his novel.

Dear Mr. Brockwell,
  I regret to inform you . . .

Another rejection letter.

Another punch to his gut.

That's what he got for trying to do something worthwhile with his life.

He shook off the petty thought, inwardly apologizing to God.

After all, it wasn't God's fault his book was not good enough. That *he* was not good enough. . . .

The words that had gone through his mind so many times over the years ran through again like a familiar refrain. The refrain of his life. He knew he had many sins to atone for, far more than one or two good deeds could overcome. He was beyond redemption.

But then the words Mrs. Reeves had spoken whispered themselves over the old familiar words, like a line of harmony. *"My dear boy, none of us deserves forgiveness. None of us can do enough good deeds to atone for our own failings. If we could, God would not have had to send the Son He loved into the world to die for us. But He did, because He loves us."*

The knowledge that he was not good enough was old news. But that the Son of God had died to save him? That the Father of all loved him? He'd heard it before, growing up with the Reeves and attending church with his own family as a child, but now it struck him as new . . . and extremely difficult to fathom.

Later that afternoon, Richard walked past the drawing room window, then turned back and peered closer. Faint white flakes dotted the air, floating gently down to earth like confectioners' sugar. A streak of boyish glee teased his stomach. Snow in the south of England was a relatively rare thing.

"Look, Justina. It's snowing."

His little sister squealed and hurried to join him at the window. A memory rushed into his mind of pulling Justina on a sled, the little girl bundled up head to foot, her dark eyes bright and an impish grin on face, rather like now.

"Oh!" she breathed. "How magical!"

The snow continued to fall, the flakes thickening into puffs of icing sugar.

They went to another window and looked out behind the house. There the branches of oak and lime trees stretched out their bare arms as though to catch the snow, their long limbs soon speckled white. The large topiary house was slowly being transformed into a fort of snow. It seemed a shame there were no children about the place to enjoy it. Susanna's children came to mind. Perhaps he would invite them to come over and play.

As the day progressed, the snow formed peaks on the veranda furniture, and glazed the small red fruits of the crab apple trees, more elegant than any display of greenery that ever decked the mantelpieces of Brockwell Court.

Richard went to his room and dressed warmly in a flannel waistcoat, trousers, greatcoat, and boots, and wrapped the muffler around his neck. He dressed Wally in his warmest woolen waistcoat, his tweed hat secured by a strap tied beneath his jaw.

Together they went outside and entered an altered world. Snow collected on the rooftops, fence rails, hedges, and signposts. It covered the walks, drive, and fountain in a white cape.

The snow clung more readily to the bushy evergreens, frosting them in a layer of Devonshire cream, which sparkled in the sunlight like diamond chips. Richard had once seen a painting of a *tannenbaum*, a traditional German Christmas tree bedecked with candles. Now observing the green branches ornamented with twinkling white light, he could understand the appeal of bringing such a tree indoors, though his mother would never allow it.

They made their way to the High Street. There he saw ladies wearing wooden pattens to raise their feet from the wet ground and protect their shoes. A few shoppers carried umbrellas to shield their heads from the falling snow. Wally, however, bounded right through it with undisguised glee.

At The Bell Inn across the street, a stagecoach arrived, its horses' manes white with snow. Snow also dusted the hats and shoulder capes of the coachman and the shivering outside passengers. A young man from the inn hurried out to offer the passengers mugs of warm mulled wine. Richard thought again of Murray taking Jamie's place on the roof and felt renewed admiration for the sacrifice, and a stab of guilt for not even considering doing so himself.

Richard turned left, down the steep hill that had given Ivy Hill its name.

He saw adults pulling small children on hand sleds or sledges, while bigger children had dug out old sleds or fashioned new ones out of boards or whatever they could find. Dozens of them coasted down the snow-covered hillside between Ivy Hill and Wishford, the best sleds among them sliding almost to the turnpike at the bottom, near the Fairmont School, where its pupils threw snow-balls at one another.

Richard found himself smiling, and warmth spread through his chest, despite the frigid temperature.

He turned and walked westward, past more snowy fields, glad for his tall, sturdy boots.

In a lonely place, he stopped, struck by the sight of a long stretch of freshly fallen snow. Unscathed by animal tracks, footprints, or wheel ruts. Untouched by man. Pure white, unblemished, unspoilt, beautiful—perfectly capturing and reflecting the sunlight.

What would it be like to be that new, that perfect, that pure, he wondered, when he himself felt sullied—a dark, muddy mire.

And what was it about seeing such a sight that made a man want to step foot across it, to claim the virgin territory for himself and make his mark? And too often, end up ruining it? Richard shook his head. Not this time. Not him, not anymore.

As Richard walked back, he met Nicholas, Justina, and Arabella dressed in their warmest coats, hats, and gloves, Justina's hands tucked inside a large fur muff.

"Richard. You couldn't resist a walk, I see," Justina greeted him.

"No, nor you."

"How could we? It is so beautiful," Arabella's gaze scanned the frosty white landscape all around them, her eyes as blue as cornflowers.

Richard asked, "May I walk with you awhile?"

"Of course."

They started up Ebsbury Road, but Justina hesitated when they reached Thornvale. "You know. I think we ought to pop in and greet your mother, Nicholas. It would be rude to pass without stopping."

"I agree," he replied.

Justina said to Richard and Arabella, "You two go ahead."

"Are you sure?"

"Yes, go on," his sister urged. "We'll catch up."

Having no desire to see the dragon-like woman he'd heard about, Richard readily agreed, and he and Arabella walked on, Wally's tail wagging nonstop.

The sun shone, warming the air, and the gentle snow suddenly changed into sleet.

When the ice pellets began striking their hat brims, Arabella cried, "Oh no!"

Richard picked up Wally with one arm and with his other grabbed Arabella's hand. Pulling her along, he ran for cover under an old holly tree. They ducked beneath its branches, dislodging snow, which slipped down his collar with an icy shock.

The red berries, glazed with snow, were a lovely sight, though the zinging balls of ice pelting them were less pleasant. The spiky leaves danced with the pellets of sleet but thankfully shielded them from the worst of the onslaught.

He looked at his companion. "All right?"

She nodded. "Quick thinking."

It was not the first time he'd taken cover under this tree with someone, but he did not say as much to her.

Snow clung to her hat and eyelashes, and her cheeks turned pink. She looked cold yet charming. The urge to kiss her, to warm her lips with his, washed over him, but he restrained himself.

He cleared his throat. "This is what we get for walking in all weather."

"I like to walk."

A gust of wind blew snow down Arabella's neck. She gasped and shivered.

"Here." He set Wally down and stepped near, putting his arm

around her shoulders, to protect her from the falling snow and sleet, he justified to himself.

Unable to resist, he drew her closer and was pleased when she did not pull away.

He quoted:

> "A whirl-blast from behind the hill
> Rushed o'er the wood with startling sound;
> Then—all at once the air was still,
> And showers of hailstones pattered round.
> Where leafless oaks towered high above,
> I sat within an undergrove
> Of tallest hollies, tall and green;
> A fairer bower was never seen. . . ."

When he'd finished, she said, "Wordsworth, right?"

He looked at her, impressed. "Very good."

His gaze was drawn to her mouth. Again came the urge to lean down and kiss her.

She shivered again, and chivalry won out.

"Here, take my coat."

"No, I couldn't."

He tugged off his outer greatcoat, the cold air biting his flesh through his wool frock coat. He settled the long garment over her shoulders, allowing his hands to linger on her arms.

Seeing the gratitude shining in her wide blue eyes, satisfaction thrummed through him. His hand reached out of its own accord and stroked her face.

"Your cheeks are like ice."

At his touch, she flashed a look up at him from beneath her lashes. What emotion did he see there? Pleasure, wariness, alarm?

He withdrew his hand. Beyond the tree, the sleet softened into snow once more, falling gently to the ground. "Come, Miss Awdry. It has let up a little. We had better hurry back while we can." To himself he added, *Before I say or do something I'll regret.*

He pushed aside the tree branch and offered her his arm. "Shall we?"

With an uncertain smile, she put her arm through his. Wally gave a bark of encouragement, and together the three of them emerged from their shelter and hurried back to Brockwell Court.

CHAPTER

TWELVE

The next morning, Richard awoke early, eagerly climbed from bed, and wrapped his dressing gown around himself against the chill of the room. He stepped to the window, folded back the shutters, and looked out.

Yes! Still white.

Icicles hung from the eaves, and he recalled sucking on them as a boy until he realized they tasted more like dirt than ices from a confectioner.

The groundsman and under gardener had cleared the walkways and drive only to have them covered again this morning. While snow itself was relatively rare in Ivy Hill, an accumulation of several inches that did not melt away quickly was rarer still.

Richard went and found his brother. "Do we still have that old sleigh?"

"Yes. At the back of the carriage house. Kept meaning to sell it to someone in the north who would get more use of it, but never did."

"Good. Think I'll make use of it myself, if you don't mind."

"Not at all."

Richard helped the groom clean up the sleigh and then, leaving the young man to harness the horse, went inside to find Arabella.

Pausing at the archway into the drawing room, he surveyed

the telling scene within. Justina and Nicholas sat over a game of draughts, talking quietly and smiling at one another at regular intervals, clearly in their own little world. Horace sat stiffly between Penelope and Arabella on the long sofa, while their mother embroidered in a chair nearby, now and again glancing surreptitiously toward the awkward trio.

Thinking quickly, Richard said, "Horace, we have two horses that need exercise, snow or not. I don't suppose you would care to oblige?"

Horace almost leapt from the sofa. "Would I! Yes, please."

Lady Lillian cleared her throat.

At the signal, Horace fiddled with his neckcloth and turned to the sisters. "That is . . . if one of you might like to accompany me?"

The two women looked at one another. Arabella opened her mouth to reply, but Richard interrupted her.

"I was hoping Miss Arabella would go for a sleigh ride with me."

"I . . ." She seemed about to refuse, but then, with a look at Penelope, said, "Yes, thank you. I have never ridden in a sleigh, if one does not count a hand sledge."

"Excellent. Dress warmly."

While she rose to comply, Horace and Penelope went to change into riding clothes, and Richard slipped upstairs for his muffler, feeling rather proud of himself. He stopped at Murray's room, guessing he would find the man at the desk, bent over quill and ink, editing the next issue of his magazine. But when he arrived at his open door, he was taken aback to see Susanna in the threshold, little Frederick in her arms, chatting cheerfully with his friend.

"Em, pardon me," he said. "Just seeing how Murray is getting on."

"Oh . . . Richard. We were just talking."

Flushing, Susanna bobbed a curtsy and turned to go. "Better get this young man back to the nursery."

Richard stroked his nephew's head as they passed. When she'd left them, Murray looked up sheepishly. "I hope you don't mind?"

Did he mind? Richard felt an odd tangle of emotions: surprise, concern, and an urge to protect.

"No. Just didn't want to leave you on your own too long, though I see I needn't have worried."

"Richard, I . . ."

He raised a palm. "No criticism intended. I promise."

His friend smiled. "Well then. Good."

A short while later, Richard and Arabella walked out the rear door to the waiting horse and sleigh. The small equipage was of old-fashioned design, with a single seat in front, like an ornate cushioned chair. Behind this was an elevated bench where the driver would perch above his passenger, his knees near her shoulders, both facing forward. It was a strangely intimate position.

The groom had secured a festive plume to the horse's head and hung bells from the harness. He thanked the young man sincerely.

Richard offered Arabella a hand to steady her. She stepped in and sat on the faded velvet seat. He laid warm bricks at her feet, wrapped a plush lap rug over her legs, and tucked it around her. He enjoyed doing so and lingered longer than absolutely necessary.

She looked self-conscious at his ministrations but did not protest.

"That should keep you warm," he said, already feeling warmer himself.

He settled onto the rear bench. Positioned slightly above her, he could see the road ahead and handle the reins without impediment.

"Perhaps later we might go into Wishford and see Jamie."

"Good idea."

He clicked the horse into motion. "Walk on."

The horse obeyed, then increased its pace, the sleigh bells jingling happily with each trotting step.

Uncertain how the sleigh might accelerate down steep Ivy Hill, Richard turned the horse in the opposite direction, passing behind the church and through the outskirts of the village. They waved to passersby as they went and saw a group of young men playing football in the snow.

They crossed Pudding Brook at the packhorse bridge, wide enough to allow the narrow sleigh to pass easily. Soon they were gliding along a quiet country lane through the surrounding farmland. Out here there was little worry of encountering an oncoming wagon or dray, but that also meant the snow on the road was not packed down as on the village streets. Instead, the wind blew the snow into drifts, and it wasn't always easy to tell if they were still on the road or not.

Arabella gripped the armrests. "Richard, slow down."

"I am trying to."

The slippery surface clearly disquieted the mare, her ears going back, and eyes wide. The sleigh runners hit a patch of ice and lurched sideways, skidding to the side of the horse. The angle and tension on the harness spooked the animal all the more.

The horse stumbled, and the sleigh slid from the road into a ditch and sank into its snow-filled snare.

They came to a sudden stop, their heads jerking forward and back again. Arabella cried out.

The horse, panicked to find itself trapped by the lodged sleigh and deep snow, whinnied and strained.

"Easy, girl. It's all right," Richard soothed. He looked with concern at his companion. Arabella's hat was askew, her ostrich feather drooping in front of her face.

"Are you all right?"

"I'm afraid my foot went through the front panel when we stopped so fast."

"Oh no. Are you injured?"

"Hurts. But probably nothing serious."

"Thunder and turf. I need to get you out of here."

"Are we irrevocably stuck?"

"I'm afraid so." Richard thought of unhitching the horse and riding to find Dr. Burton, but he could not leave Miss Awdry sitting alone in the snow.

From his higher perch, Richard looked across the road and saw a house. His momentary relief instantly faded.

Bramble Cottage.

Of all the places to become stuck, why did it have to be there?

Richard hesitated. Everything in him wanted to look away. To keep his promise to his younger self that he would never step foot inside Bramble Cottage. But for all his faults, he was a gentleman and could not leave Arabella outside.

He climbed from his perch, and bent low. "Put your arms around my neck."

"Oh. I am sure I could walk." She extracted her half boot from the new hole in the footboard and winced. "Maybe . . ."

"Better not risk it." Slipping an arm behind her back and the other beneath her knees, he lifted Arabella with effort. Straining, he carried her up the incline, a grunt escaping him.

"Am I too heavy?" she asked, face stricken in embarrassment. "Put me down and I'll walk."

"No. No problem," he panted, forcing his feet toward Bramble Cottage. He was grateful now for all the boxing and fencing he'd done at his club or he'd be even less fit to carry damsels through snowbanks.

He was also glad Susanna had mentioned that Mrs. Haverhill had moved away. His family had long owned the place, and he assumed they still did, so felt few qualms about entering on that score. He recalled where the key to the door used to be kept. Would it still be there after all this time? He set Arabella down a moment. "Here, lean against the wall. Don't put too much weight on that foot."

"Sorry. I have eaten a great deal of sweets since coming to Brockwell Court. I probably broke your back."

"Not a bit of it. You are absolutely perfect."

"Hardly. No one can claim that."

"Certainly not I."

He knocked on the door, just to be sure. "Halloo? Anyone home?"

He extracted the key from the flowerpot and unlocked the door.

"How did you . . . ? Are you sure you should do that?"

"We own the cottage, or at least I think we still do. The former tenant has moved on."

"Oh."

Richard pushed open the door and looked inside. Unreality blurred his vision. For a moment he was twelve years old again, staring in the window, then turning and running through the woods, tears streaming down his face.

He picked up Arabella and carried her across the threshold.

In the main room, he set her on a sofa near the hearth. The previous tenant had left the place fully furnished. He pulled a blanket from the back, shook it out, and laid it across her shoulders.

"Th-thank you."

He hesitated. "I could leave the door open, if you wish. For propriety's sake."

"And let the cold wind inside?" She shook her head. "I'll risk the gossip. Unless you are worried about your own reputation?"

"Ha-ha. Everyone already thinks me a reprobate. But you are admired and respected here."

She tilted her head, regarding him in some surprise. "You are kind to think of my reputation at such a time."

Richard looked away from her wide eyes. Glancing around the room, he observed to himself, "Very little has changed."

"You have been in here before?" she asked.

"Never."

She looked at him in confusion, but he made no reply. His gaze landed on the cold hearth. "There is still a little wood and a lump of coal." He looked atop the mantel and found an old tinderbox, complete with fire striker, flint, and remnant of char cloth. Now if only he could successfully light it without making a fool of himself. Servants had always lit his fires. Sinking to his knees, he struck the steel against the flint, and lo and behold, sparks fell onto the cloth. With gentle blowing, he was able to conjure a small fire, feeding it kindling and then one of the logs, which would hopefully soon warm the room.

In the meantime, he found another blanket in the wardrobe and laid it over her knees.

"Will you be all right on your own for a few minutes? I am going to try to unharness the horse. I saw a little shed beside the house."

"Yes, go. I'll be all right here."

It took longer than he'd imagined, but he finally managed to release the horse from its traces and then led the jittery animal into the small shed and out of the wind. "There you go, girl. Rest here for a while."

He returned to the cottage and knelt before Arabella. She looked so pretty, cheeks pink, her golden hair in tendrils around her face, having come loose at impact. He forced his attention to her boot. "Do you mind if I take a look at your foot?"

"I . . . I suppose it would be wise to survey the damage. Throbs awfully, but my half boots offered some protection. These frilly gloves are useless however. My fingers are stiff with cold, so I doubt I can manage the laces."

"I'll give it a go."

He removed his leather gloves, cupped his hands together, and blew on his fingers. Then he undid the bow and began loosening the laces. It took him back to Justina's childhood and the many times he had helped his little sister on or off with her little half boots or had retied her laces when one came loose. They had often ridden together, gone exploring, or taken off their boots to wade in Pudding Brook.

"What has you smiling like that?" she asked.

He glanced up. "You won't believe me, but I was thinking of Justina. I used to help her like this when she was little." He met her veiled gaze and saw her skepticism. "Though with my reputation, you probably assumed the worst."

She looked away, her blush confirming his suspicions.

Boot unlaced, Richard gingerly grasped the heel and eased it off her foot.

She grimaced.

"Sorry. Am I hurting you?"

"No, I just thought of my stocking. You'll have to turn your back so I can roll it down."

"Of course."

But when the boot was removed, they saw the toe of the stocking had been torn away, and her big toe and the next protruded through the hole.

"It wasn't like that this morning. Please don't think I make a habit of wearing torn stockings, Mr. Brockwell. I know you are fastidious in all points of sartorial elegance."

Humor glimmered in her eyes, and he guessed she was teasing him to lighten the awkward moment. He grinned. "Indeed I am. And this torn stocking offends me. Will you mind terribly if I tear it further to get a better view?"

"No, you may not! Stockings are dear, and this one may yet be mended. Close your eyes and let me take it off."

"Oh, very well." He sighed and closed his eyes.

"By the way," she said, "it isn't fair you have such long eyelashes. Now, no peeking."

"On my honor." Was he a man of honor? Richard wondered. He was about to be tested.

He heard the rustle of fabric and dutifully kept his eyes closed. "There."

He opened his eyes, his gaze lifting to her flushed face. "You are lovely when you blush."

Then he adopted his best professional demeanor and studied her foot. A delicate thing. Small, elegant. Shapely ankles . . . He swallowed and looked at her toes instead. Less to admire there. The big toe and its compatriot were already swollen and turning an unbecoming shade of purple.

He ran his fingers over the swelling skin. "Can you move them?" She did so.

He made a face. "Puts one in mind of monkey toes."

"Mr. Brockwell! You are not gallant."

"Sometimes humor is best."

"I agree."

"No obvious breaks or bleeding. That's a good sign, but I'd like the doctor to take a look."

"Perhaps you have missed your calling."

"Me, a blood-and-bones man?" He shuddered theatrically. "Horrors. Just seeing your ghastly purple toes is enough to put me off the profession."

"Ha-ha."

A knock sounded at the door, startling them both. A small voice called, "Mr. Brockwell?"

Richard went to the door and opened it to Peter, Susanna's son.

"I saw your sleigh fall into the ditch. Are you all right?"

"Yes." His gestured to his companion. "Though Miss Awdry here has hurt her foot. Might you stay with her while I try to find the doctor?"

"I'll go. I'm much faster than you. Besides, Dr. Burton is with my grandmamma right now."

"Excellent."

"Won't take long," the boy added. "You ought to have brought her to our house in the first place."

"I didn't think I could carry her that far."

The boy nodded sagely. "You are old, after all. I shall be back in a trice."

Richard stifled a retort. "Thank you, Peter."

He ran off, and Richard returned to Arabella.

"What a kind little boy, except for calling you old. How do you know him?" she asked.

"His mother is Susanna, our new nurserymaid."

"Ah . . ." She lifted her chin, that same suspicion shadowing her face.

Richard sat beside her to wait, surprised when she spread the blanket over him as well.

"Thank you. Actually, that's not fair," he amended. "Susanna was my friend long before she came into our employ."

"Your friend?"

"Yes. Both her and her brother. Susanna and I were the same

age and Seth a year older. They lived in Honeycroft, in the woods not far from here. They were all kindness itself to me as boy. Accepted me, almost as one of their family." Under the blanket, he reached for her hand. "Your fingers are still cold." He held them, gratified when she did not pull away.

"But you had a family of your own."

"I did. But there was something special about theirs. Loving, affectionate, good-natured . . . Whereas my own parents . . . Well, that was not always the case." He shifted on the sofa, quickly diverting the topic. "And what about your parents? Was their marriage a happy one?"

"Yes. There was quite an age difference between them, but they were thoroughly devoted to one another. My mother misses Papa every day, and so do I."

Richard nodded his understanding. "I'm sorry. When I heard Mr. Reeves died, I felt true loss."

"How long ago did he die?"

"About two years. I should have come back for the funeral, but I didn't. If I had, I might have realized earlier that Mrs. Reeves had fallen on hard times." He slowly shook his head, guilt lancing him. "I should have guessed. After all, she had lost her husband and her only son. Nothing was the same after Seth died. Susanna married and moved away, and I . . ."

"You?"

"Let us just say I have regrets where the Reeveses are concerned. And especially where Susanna is concerned." He did not try to defend himself. Arabella knew his reputation, and he doubted she would believe that he no longer trifled with young ladies' affections. Why should she?

He looked at Arabella, heart beating dully within him. She really was too good for him. "I have regrets where you are concerned as well. I have been insufferably rude and have not treated you as I ought."

"Perhaps, but you have not injured me. I know I followed you around like a loyal pup as a girl—you no doubt took pains to avoid me. And you vexed me no end when you made insolent remarks about my sister." She added on a teasing note, "Oh, I wanted to injure *you* then, but you did not injure me."

Richard, however, remained somber.

"And Susanna . . . How does she feel about you now?" Arabella asked. "Have you ever apologized to her?"

"I have, but she has not forgiven me, and I don't blame her. Her life has not been easy."

She looked at him closely. Too closely. "You love her, I think."

Richard stared into the cold hearth and answered truthfully, "I will always love her, as I loved her brother and parents. But I am not in love with her, nor she with me."

"If you say so."

"I do." Richard looked around again and heaved a sigh. "I can't believe I'm sitting here, in Bramble Cottage."

"Why?"

"It is a place of bad associations. But let's leave off with ancient history. There is no use in dredging up the past. It can only hurt people."

"Sounds like whatever it was hurt you already."

"Me?" He stared at her. "I am not in any pain. I am my own man. Free to live and do as I please. I could not be happier."

"If you say so," she said again.

He rose and placed a pillow under her foot, added another piece of wood to the fire, and then looked out the window. "Peter and the doctor should be here any moment."

"I am all right, Mr. Brockwell. Do sit down."

But he kept pacing. "It's a lovely cottage, really. With a little work, perhaps a modest addition, it could be quite comfortable. One could write a great many books in such a snug cottage."

"Do you think so?"

"I imagine so, yes." He cleared his throat. "Though I am, of course, no novelist."

Richard looked around him. It was a pleasant house, and the views from the windows were peaceful and bucolic. Could he write in such a place, or would the memories always haunt him?

He asked, "Can I get you anything? Another blanket? Shall I see if I can find any water? A pump?"

"No, I am well. Don't worry." She looked up at him, a teasing smile on her lips. "You know, you take good care of a lady, for a determined bachelor."

Discomfited at her praise, he rubbed the back of his neck. "Well . . . don't want your sister coming after me, do I?" He winked, and she tossed a pillow at him.

A short while later, Dr. Burton arrived. Discerning no break or sprain, he wrapped her foot for support and prescribed rest and willow bark tea for the pain. Then he and Richard conveyed Arabella safely back to Brockwell Court in his cart.

When her mother had finished fussing over her, and Arabella convinced her sister she was perfectly well and just wanted to lie down and rest for a time, Arabella was finally left alone in the guest room.

She wanted time to reflect. To rehearse and make sense of all that had transpired between her and Mr. Brockwell over the last few days.

First that romantic walk in the snow that had turned to sleet. Ducking under the holly tree with him. Hidden from view. All alone in the world or so it seemed . . . if one did not count his dog.

He had stroked her cheek and looked deeply into her eyes. Then his gaze had shifted to her mouth. She was certain he'd wanted to kiss her, and heaven help her, she'd wanted him to.

She thought next of the ill-fated sleigh ride, remembering how he'd picked her up and carried her inside. She had wrapped her hands around his neck and would like an excuse to do so once more.

After setting her gently down, he had lit a fire and made sure she was warm enough. He'd knelt before her and honorably closed his eyes while she removed her stocking, long dark eyelashes fanning against his cheek. So handsome. So gentlemanlike.

That thought gave her pause. *Richard Brockwell, gentlemanlike?*

No, Arabella! she argued within herself. Don't idolize the man. And don't forget—you know his true nature. As does Susanna, by the sound of it.

Instead, she thought of how easily he'd removed a feminine boot, grinning as he did so, and saying brazenly *"With my reputation, you probably assumed the worst."*

She *had* thought he'd been recalling undressing a lover. He'd had lovers, she did not doubt, and felt uneasy at the thought. Was he really the libertine many people thought him?

Again she recalled his sultry gaze and heard his warm, sensual voice in her ear. *"You are lovely when you blush."*

She tried to dislodge the image from her mind's eye. *Don't fall under his seductive powers!*

And yet . . . he'd had his chance there in the deserted cottage. What better opportunity to attempt to take liberties if he'd wanted to? But he had behaved in a gentlemanlike manner. Except, perhaps, for roasting her about her unattractive toes.

He could have taken advantage of their private moment to at least try to kiss her, but instead he'd told her about the Reeves family and his friendship with Susanna. His words and troubled expression remained vivid in her mind. *"Let us just say I have regrets . . . especially where Susanna is concerned."*

He had not given details, but he had clearly disappointed Susanna somehow. And would no doubt disappoint *her* as well, given the opportunity. He'd said, *"She has not forgiven me, and I don't blame her."*

Forgiven him for what? Arabella wondered. She could guess. He was a reputed rake after all. But his feelings for Susanna seemed far more serious than a casual seduction.

Arabella reminded herself that she knew his unflattering, ungentlemanlike secret. At least one of them. She'd been a guest in Brockwell Court years ago when he was nineteen and she sixteen. The others had gone out hunting, but she stayed back to read. Hearing voices, she'd peeked into the passage. His father stood at the door to his bedchamber, voice raised in anger. Richard had been sent down from Oxford and since his return had been caught trifling with a housemaid.

And now Richard had arranged to have pretty Susanna hired on as a maid at Brockwell Court. She'd seen them talking together in clandestine fashion already. What was the truth: Were they really just friends, or were they having an affair? She was a widow after all, and Richard Brockwell was known to have a penchant for pretty widows. Or did he deeply love Susanna?

And which would be harder to bear?

Sometime later, Justina came in to see how she fared. Standing by Arabella's bed, the younger woman clasped her hands together. "I am so sorry this happened. Especially during our party and in our sleigh."

"Don't worry. I am all right. Just resting."

"I do hope this won't spoil your evening. It is New Year's Eve, after all."

She gave Justina a plucky smile. "I shan't let it spoil anything."

"Good." At the sound of voices from outside, Justina turned to the window.

Arabella heard both adult and childish voices along with peals of laughter. Curious, she asked, "Who is it?"

"Richard and Mr. Murray and two children. I'm not sure who. All bundled up as they are, it is difficult to see."

Arabella rose and walked gingerly across the room, her ankle sore but steady.

Justina turned her head. "Are you sure you are all right to walk?"

Biting her lip against the pain, Arabella said, "Perfectly."

She joined Justina at the window. In the back garden, two children darted in and out of the snow-covered topiary house—a boy and a little girl in woolen coats. The boy's grinning face appeared in the topiary "door" as he hurled a snowball at Richard, who deftly dodged it. Arabella recognized the boy as Peter, who'd fetched the doctor to Bramble Cottage. Susanna's son. Richard tossed a snowball back, but the boy ducked inside the shelter and evaded him.

"Richard and I used to play like that," Justina breathed, her expression wistful.

Susanna appeared below, likely finished in the nursery for the day, and came out to collect her children. The young girl ran toward her, and Susanna bent to receive her embrace. The child giggled and sneaked snow down her mother's neck. Susanna squealed like a schoolgirl and bent to pick up a handful of retribution. She threw it at her fleeing daughter, missed, and hit Richard in the back. Or had it been purposeful? Richard laughed and chased the little girl, lifting her high in the air, while Mr. Murray turned and threw a snowball at Susanna.

"Those must be our nurserymaid's children," Justina said. "Richard mentioned he might invite them. I wish we could join them."

"Go ahead. Don't let me stop you."

"Perhaps I shall. If you are certain there is nothing you need."

"Not a thing. I promise."

"Very well." Justina squeezed Arabella's hand, eyes bright. "Rest up. It shall be a late night."

When she had gone, Arabella returned her attention to the scene of playful affection outside. She didn't see Mr. Murray any longer. He must have gone in. But there were Richard, Susanna, and the children. The four of them looked like a family. Arabella's stomach pinched at the thought. And once more, Richard's words whispered in her mind, *"I will always love her."*

Arabella turned away.

She took a deep breath and squared her shoulders, telling herself it did not matter. Yes, he was handsome, almost painfully so. Yes, she was attracted to him, and, she believed, he was attracted to her. But none of that changed the fact she had plans for her life that did not include marriage, and certainly not marriage to a man attached to someone else. A man she could not trust.

No. Arabella resolved anew to stay the course. To keep her distance and avoid being alone with him in the future.

CHAPTER

THIRTEEN

While Arabella rested and after Susanna and her children returned home, Richard rode into Wishford to see Jamie. The boy was too busy to talk for more than a few minutes. He looked less weary now that his nightly terrorizer was gone, though he still flinched whenever Mr. Knock came near. If only that rat could be dealt with as easily as the other.

Late that afternoon, everyone dressed warmly and gathered in the hall. Mr. and Mrs. Bingley, who had hosted elderly relatives over Christmas, had invited everyone to their house for New Year's Eve.

The bell was rung, and the carriages spoken for. The guests talked amicably amongst themselves while awaiting the three vehicles that would carry them to Stapleford: the Brockwells' barouche-landau, the Awdrys' coach, and the Bingleys' carriage.

The first vehicle rattled to the door. Lady Barbara, always first on such occasions, was carefully attended to the Brockwells' barouche-landau by Sir Timothy and Mr. Ashford, followed by Rachel and Justina.

As he entered, Timothy directed the coachman, "The roads don't seem slippery, but just in case one of us has trouble, keep as much together with the other carriages as you can."

"Very good, sir."

The Awdrys' coach pulled up next. Lady Lillian stepped in first, and her daughter Penelope followed. Horace eagerly stepped in behind her.

That left Arabella, Richard, and Mr. Murray awaiting the Bingleys' carriage. When it drew up, Mr. Murray opened the door and offered Arabella a hand in. Richard followed her inside and sat across from her.

Then Murray hesitated. Instead of stepping in, he shut the door and hurriedly wedged himself into the Awdrys' coach.

Arabella's mouth parted in surprise. She leaned toward the window to see what became of him.

"Crafty fellow," Richard murmured, then looked at her. "I hope you don't mind a tête-à-tête drive?"

She hesitated, expression discomposed. "I . . . suppose not."

An awkward moment of silence passed, broken only by the rumble of wheels and jingle of tack as the horses trotted onward. Outside, twilight fell, but light from candle lamps on either side of the coach illuminated their faces.

Clearly nervous, Arabella began speaking with gravity of the weather and how kind it was of the Bingleys to invite them to their home.

Richard bit back a grin. "Very propitious, I agree."

"How unfortunate that my brother and new sister were delayed in returning from their wedding trip," she said.

"Is it unfortunate? Would not one wish for a longer wedding trip?"

"That depends, I suppose, on whether one is prepared for such a delay, with sufficient funds and clean clothing. And, after all, one wishes to be with family at Christmas."

"So I have been told."

She tilted her head to one side. "You have not been home for Christmas in some time, I recollect. I hope you are enjoying yourself?"

"I am. Especially at this moment."

"You did not attend Cyril and Miss Bingley's wedding."

"No, I did not have that pleasure."

"Do you not like weddings?"

"Not especially."

"I suppose, as a bachelor, they remind you of what you don't have."

Richard considered. "If your theory is correct, then you must not like weddings either."

"On the contrary, I do. I may have chosen to devote my life to charitable works, but that does not mean I cannot celebrate with others who choose a more traditional path."

"Do you really mean not to marry?"

She turned toward him, lamplight flickering on one side of her face. "Why do you sound so surprised, when you are determined to remain single as well?"

It was a question Richard was not quite prepared to answer, so instead he changed the subject. "Would you mind if I sat beside you? I feel a little ill facing backward."

"Oh. No, of course not."

He moved over. Sitting side by side, their elbows and knees occasionally brushed as the coach turned a corner or jostled over a bump.

"Are you warm enough?" he asked.

"Yes," she said, with a little shiver.

"Here." He lifted a sheepskin from the opposite bench and spread it over them both. "That's better. Very kind of the Bingleys to think of it."

"Th-thank you."

The coachman turned a sharp corner, and the movement tipped Arabella closer to him.

"Sorry," she murmured.

"Don't be. It's warmer this way."

Shoulder to shoulder, Richard finally settled on his answer. "You, Miss Awdry, should marry—but only a man who deserves you. One who would treat you with the utmost respect and adoration."

She turned to look at him and asked softly, "Do you know of any such man?"

Richard stilled. The moment was there. The opportunity ripe. All he had to do was say the words, then lean forward. In the half light of the coach, their faces were mere inches apart. It would be so easy to kiss her. . . .

His gaze lingered on her eyes, then dropped to her mouth. Her beguiling, innocent mouth. Then he leaned back with a sigh. "Unfortunately not."

Solemnly, she said, "And you are not he."

"Is that a statement or a question?"

"I would never marry a man who would not be faithful to me."

"And you believe I would not be faithful to you?"

"I . . . doubt it."

He thought, then said, "The night you arrived, you told me you have kept a secret of mine for a decade now. Will you tell me what it was?"

Embarrassed, she shook her head.

"Well, I can guess. Not sure if you overheard something or how you learnt of it, but either way, I know I can trust you not to repeat this." He took a breath, then said, "My own father was not faithful to my mother. For a time, I took that as license. Casted off moral scruples and followed in his footsteps. After all, I thought, what's good for the gander is good for the gosling.

"But I've had to reconsider my conclusions and take a hard look at my life. The truth is, I detested that my father kept a mistress— that he betrayed my mother, betrayed his family. Men can say all they like about secrets between gentlemen and 'that's just what men do,' but I know firsthand how it injures the children. I would never do that to mine. That is why I will never marry . . . unless there is genuine love and fidelity—all or nothing."

Arabella blinked. "I'm sorry. That must have been very difficult." She inhaled a long breath. "Do you think you *could* be faithful to one woman?"

He pondered. "Yes. I did not think I would ever want to. But you, Miss Awdry, have changed my mind. Unfortunately, I am not good enough for you."

"Are you the best judge of that?"

He pushed his hand through his hair. "You judged it yourself the first night of the party. You called me a heartless libertine. And you were right."

"I thought . . . perhaps . . . you were changing?"

Should he tell her he'd mended his ways years ago—had never again pressed his advantage with an innocent young woman? Then what was he doing now? How could he tell her he'd changed, when everything in him wanted to take her in his arms right then and there, propriety be hanged?

Instead, he leaned away. "Do you think a man can change his nature?"

"With God's help, yes."

Through the coach windows, the Bingley home came into view. Lanterns lit the drive, and candles glowed in every window of the manor house. Their private tête-à-tête was about to come to an end. Their privacy and his opportunity with it. Was he making a mistake?

Regardless, it was too late. The carriage stopped, and a liveried footman appeared to let down the step.

Arabella looked away to hide her disappointment. *Foolish creature*, she chastised herself. Was she truly disappointed he had not offered to marry her, or kissed her? Had she forgotten her plans and his reputation, not to mention the precedent his father had set?

She vaguely realized he'd been trying to distance himself for her sake, but in this instance, she had not wanted him to be noble. She'd wanted him to kiss her, but he had not. Yet she was certain he'd wanted to.

They alighted. Donning a placid smile, she laid a cool hand on Richard's offered arm. Her injured toes ached with each step. She could walk well enough, but hoped no dancing was planned for the evening.

Stepping inside, servants took their coats, capes, and mantles.

In the great hall, they were welcomed by their hosts, Mr. and Mrs. Bingley.

The evening party commenced. Card tables had been set up in the drawing room, and guests sat in groups of four to play whist. Though not fond of cards, Arabella politely took part. Later, Mrs. Bingley suggested parlour games for the younger people.

After charades and a memory game, they next played Buffy Gruffy. For this game, a blindfolded player stood in the center of a circle of chairs. The other players changed places as silently as possible. The blindfolded person advanced, arms outstretched until reaching someone. Then he or she asked three questions to try to guess the person's identity. The players had to answer truthfully but tried to disguise their voices, often teasing the blindfolded player as well. It was a game Arabella had played eagerly as a younger woman but now with some trepidation.

The game began with the usual blind blunders, embarrassing questions, and silly voices. Then it was Richard's turn. Blindfolded, he advanced toward Arabella. She sat quietly, hoping he would come to her and fearing it at the same time.

Hands outstretched, his fingers found her ears, the curls at her temples, then her warm cheeks. Arabella's pulse began to accelerate.

"Is your hair fair?" he asked.

She answered in her best imitation of an old crone. "Yes, young man, it is."

"Are your eyes as blue as cornflowers?"

"Almost as blue as yours."

"Are you . . . attracted to anyone here?"

She started at the unexpected question, but answered truthfully. "Yes."

Voice husky, he asked, "Who?"

She licked dry lips. "Sorry. That is four questions."

The games continued for a time, and then the players paused to take refreshment. Needing a respite from all the chattering people,

Richard excused himself, walking alone across the great hall and into the library. Ah, the company of books was far more to his liking.

After breathing in the scents of leather, musty pages, and ink for a time, he would be ready to rejoin society.

A few solitary, silent moments passed. Then in the passage beyond the library he heard voices. Arabella's voice and her sister's lower one, talking in confidential tones.

"What is wrong, Pen? Did Mr. Bingley say something to upset you?"

"I . . ."

"My dear, what is it?"

"It's . . . I-I could be wrong, but I think he wants to . . . propose. Marriage. To me."

"I should hope so!"

"Do you? You don't mind?"

"Of course I don't mind. I've long known he admires you and wondered why he hesitated."

"I feared it was . . . because of you."

"Me?" Arabella's voice rose in surprise.

"He did dance with you first and paid you attention over Christmas. . . ."

"Did he? Well, perhaps a little, but I assumed he was just being kind to his future sister-in-law."

"No. His mother urged him to try. He confessed as much to me yesterday. Mrs. Bingley prefers you, because you are so pretty and ladylike and accomplished . . ."

"Oh no. I am sorry to hear it, my love. But Horace prefers you and always has. Wise man!"

Richard heard a sniff. "So he has tried to reassure me. But I worried about you. If you thought—"

"No, Pen. I never thought Horace admired me."

"That is what he thinks. He told his mother that he is done trying and at any rate Richard Brockwell is interested in you now."

"And how did Mrs. Bingley respond to that?"

"I shouldn't repeat it."

"Please do."

Standing there in the shadows, Richard steeled himself for a blow.

"She said, 'Richard Brockwell is a prodigal and a profligate. I doubt his interest is honorable. What can he offer her? He might be handsome, but as our eldest son and heir, you have far more to offer a lady.'"

Richard winced. The words were sobering and painful to hear. They were also true.

Arabella replied, "All I'll say to that is that she is right about the merits of her son. I believe you and Horace are perfectly suited, and I am thoroughly happy for you both."

"I begin to believe you."

Arabella chuckled. "As well you should!"

"And what do you think? Is Richard's interest in you honorable?"

A moment of silence followed, and Richard held his breath to better hear.

"I wonder that myself. But I have no plans to marry, as you know," Arabella said. "Now, shall we rejoin the others?"

After a late supper and tea, the party quieted down, and the carriages were summoned to take the guests home. Horace would be staying with his family for a few days but promised to return to Brockwell Court in time for the season-concluding Twelfth Night party.

To prevent the Bingleys' carriage from having to make the return trip, especially as Horace was staying home, the Brockwells and their guests crammed into the two remaining carriages. Six and four. Lady Barbara, Lady Lillian, Sir Timothy, Rachel, Justina, and Mr. Ashford rode in the larger Brockwell vehicle, and Richard, Mr. Murray, Arabella, and Penelope rode in the Awdrys' coach, the two men facing backward as the sisters faced forward.

Arabella met Richard's gaze by lamplight.

"Are you feeling all right, Mr. Brockwell?" she asked. "I can switch with you, if you like. On the way here, you mentioned facing backward makes you ill."

"Did I say that? How odd. I have never been ill a day in my life. It must have been an excuse to sit beside you."

She sucked in a surprised breath. "You schemer!"

He smirked. "Yes, I admit it. It was just an excuse to sit beside you."

"I don't know whether to be flattered or offended. I wish you would simply tell the truth. How can a lady decide whether or not to trust you?"

Richard flippantly replied, "I would not if I were you. It's a gamble, to be sure. I'd advise you to err on the side of caution." He adjusted his cravat, looking more like the dandy who'd arrived from London than the man she'd come to know since.

Mr. Murray spoke up. "He talks a good game, Miss Awdry, but I have been acquainted with Richard Brockwell for years. He may not be a gentleman in every sense, but he has his own moral code. He would never trifle with a marriageable young lady. In fact, he avoids them like the plague."

Arabella released a dry puff of laughter. "Again, I don't know whether to be flattered or offended!"

Mr. Murray amended, "All I am saying, and rather poorly, is that you, Miss Awdry, can trust Richard Brockwell completely."

"You give me too much credit, Murray," Richard said dryly. "She will think me a monk."

Arabella leveled a look at him. "I would never think that."

He avoided her gaze. Something was different, she realized. What had precipitated his return to more glib, superficial ways? Whatever it was, she didn't like it. She'd wrongly imagined he viewed her differently from other "marriageable young ladies" and had foolishly thought he might have changed.

Arabella looked at her sister instead. She was even quieter than usual. Had Mr. Bingley changed his mind, or had his mother said something to upset her?

She leaned close and whispered, "Are you all right, Pen?"

"I hardly know."

"Did Mr. Bingley . . . ?"

Pen nodded. "He asked me to marry him. Just before we left."

Arabella sucked in a breath. "That is excellent news!"

Her sister's smile flashed before she self-consciously ducked her head.

"How did you answer him?"

"I . . . I think I accepted. At least, I hope I did."

Arabella laughed. "Oh, Pen! You must make him very certain of your answer the next time you see him."

Penelope looked up, and a rare girlish giggle escaped her. "I shall indeed."

CHAPTER

FOURTEEN

Richard awoke as dawn began painting the sky. Thunder and turf. What was happening to him? He never rose this early, and certainly not after a late night. But toss and turn as he might, he could not fall back asleep.

He realized it was the first of January, the day many people began the new year with a thorough cleaning. A time for "Out with the old, in with the new."

Could Richard do the same to his heart, his ways? He hoped so. *God in heaven, give me strength. Help me become a better man.*

Giving up on sleep, he rolled from bed and quickly dressed himself in the nearest clothes at hand—a plain grey coat, and the trousers and shirt he had worn for repairs, freshly returned from the laundress.

He opened his door. The house was quiet, too quiet. Even Wally slept on.

Grabbing his greatcoat from its peg, he slipped downstairs and out the rear door, then walked behind the house and around the church, not turning up the path to Honeycroft as he often did, but instead continuing on to Bramble Cottage.

He found an old tree stump and sat down, looking at the cottage and searching his heart.

In his mind's eye, he saw himself at twelve, bending to see through the partially opened window. Cupping his hand to the glass and witnessing his father embrace a stranger.

The familiar voice had slipped through the opening. "My darling, Georgiana. What heaven it is to come here after hours trapped in a house with a shrewish wife and rebellious son."

The scene changed, and he was standing before his father's desk years later, his father as livid as he had ever seen him. "I cannot believe a son of mine has been sent down from Oxford. And now this incident with the housemaid? Is this how we've raised you, to be a lascivious, immoral wastrel?"

"That's rather hypocritical coming from you, is it not? Like father, like son, and all that."

His father grew still, his fury freezing into something hard and flintlike. "What are you talking about?"

"You know very well. The ladybird you keep in your little love nest in Bramble Cottage. Your *darling Georgiana.*"

Sir Justin's face turned purple, his lip curled and his hand fisted. Richard thought his father would strike him—indeed he believed the older man barely resisted. Instead, he locked the door and said, "Shut your mouth, you impudent, ungrateful boy. If your mother finds out, it will break her heart and ruin our marriage, and that will be on your head."

Richard held his gaze. "No, Father, it will be on yours. I am not the one who has been unfaithful to her."

The sound of footsteps now startled him. Richard turned and saw Susanna approaching up the road.

Her face fell. "Oh. Richard. I thought you were someone else."

He glanced from her cape to her gloved hands. "You're up early. On your way to Brockwell Court, I imagine?"

She nodded. For a moment, she said nothing more. Just came and stood silently beside him, near but not too close. Then she gestured toward Bramble Cottage. "I suppose you are remembering your father."

"Yes."

"Have you ever forgiven him?"

He shook his head. "Right now, I'm more concerned about you forgiving me. I let things go too far. I knew better, knew you trusted me. Afterward, you had every reason to expect an offer of marriage, but instead I simply returned to university. I hated myself for what I'd done. I did come back to apologize a few months later, when my conscience caught up with me. Did your mother tell you of my visit? I wanted to make sure you were all right. Instead, I was stunned to learn that you had married and gone to live on the coast. I felt terrible. First your mother lost her son, then her daughter married and moved away, and I was partly to blame for that. I know your life has not been easy either. Your husband dying and leaving you with two children to raise on your own."

Susanna nodded. "Thank you. I can't deny it's been hard." She opened her mouth to say more, then changed her mind and turned to the road. "Well, I had better hurry, or I'll be late."

Richard rose. "May I walk with you?"

"I . . . suppose."

They walked back the way Richard had come. A thread of tension hung heavy between them. He could tell she was still angry with him. Was she waiting for him to make amends? To apologize again? Or something else? Something . . . more?

They reached the manor's side garden, then rounded the back of the house. They were almost there. He didn't have much time.

He paused beside the topiary house. "I truly am sorry, Susanna. I know I failed you in the past, and I am trying to make things right. When I told you I was sorry before, you didn't seem to believe me. But I am."

She stopped and turned to him, eyes round with incredulity. "Words are too easy, especially for a man like you. You want to make things right. How? More than ten years have passed. Your chance to do your duty, to do right by me, have passed too. Unless . . ." She lifted her chin and sent him a challenging look. "Are you saying you would marry me now?"

His heart thudded. Weight pressed on his chest, making it hard to breathe.

Would he? It would mean disappointing, even alienating his family. It would mean giving up his own hopes and desires. Giving up Arabella.

Was this what God wanted him to do? Was this the way to forgiveness? To redemption? Yes, he would always love his old friend, yet everything in him wanted to say no.

Instead, he dropped to one knee.

Looking up, he dragged his gaze to hers. She waited, searching his face, eyes intense.

He opened his mouth to say the words.

"Stand up, Richard," Susanna said. "You don't want to marry me, and I don't want to marry you. It's all right. I don't want to live in the past anymore. We are both different people than we were all those years ago. I am growing fond of someone else now, and so are you."

She extended her hand and helped him up. He rose on legs that felt rather unstable.

"But thank you for being willing," she added. "You can go, conscience clear. You offered; I said no. You are free."

"Are you sure? I do care for you, Susanna, though I know I hurt you. Disappointed you."

"Yes, you did. I can't deny it." She sighed. "I don't blame you for what happened between us, wrong though it was. We were both grieving Seth's death and trying to comfort one another. But I did not expect you to run off afterward. That did hurt me. Thankfully, the pain did not last long. You won't like hearing it, but God used you in my life. After you left, Mr. Evans and I fell in love, and we had several happy years together."

"I am glad."

"I lost him, but that is not your fault." Susanna took a deep breath. "I . . . forgive you, Richard. I should have forgiven you long ago, but I do now. With my whole heart."

"I don't deserve it, but I appreciate it."

"Perhaps it is time you forgave your father . . . and yourself too."

"Sounds like something your mother said to me."

"Not surprising." She managed a wobbly grin. "She is a wise woman."

He took her hand and held it to his lips for a long moment. "God bless you, Susanna."

Tears glinted in her eyes. "And you, Richard."

A door opened nearby, and Susanna took a step back. Both of them turned toward the house. David Murray had come outside, looking uneasily from one to the other.

Susanna waved to him, then raised an index finger, gesturing for him to wait one minute.

She explained, "Mr. Murray has taken to greeting me when I come to work and sometimes walks me home afterward. When I first saw you outside Bramble Cottage, I thought you might be him. Mr. Murray is . . . Well, he shows every sign of becoming attached to . . . the area. Though he worries you won't approve."

"How can I not? David Murray is superior to me in every way that counts, except sartorially." Richard managed a weak grin, though his emotions were muddled.

"I should argue with you," she said. "But as I am smitten with Mr. Murray, I have no wish to. And now you are free to court that pretty Miss Awdry who so clearly admires you."

He shook his head. "She would not have me."

"Have you asked her?"

"Well, not directly."

"What does that mean?"

"I broached the topic, but she said she would never marry a man who would not be faithful to her."

"Can't blame a woman for that. So be faithful to her."

"She wouldn't give me that chance."

"You don't know that. You have always been good with words, Richard. Tell her how you really feel. Write it down if you have to."

When he said nothing, she squeezed his hand once more. "I

want you to be happy, Richard. And I want to be happy too. And with your friend, I think I have every chance of being so."

"Has he proposed?"

"Not yet. He is not exactly in a position to marry presently. Financially, I mean. His business is struggling. But I hope, eventually, we may marry."

"So do I. He's a good man. And a blessed man, if he has won your love."

Susanna leaned up on tiptoe and kissed his cheek. Then she smiled at him—the prettiest smile he had ever seen.

"He has indeed."

Richard wrapped his arms around her and held her close one last time, his heart bidding his old friend and the past good-bye.

When Arabella folded back her shutters and looked out on a new day and a new year, she was surprised to see two people standing in the garden behind the house. Richard and the pretty maid, Susanna.

The two were talking earnestly together by dawn's light, then Richard raised her hand to his lips and kissed it, holding on far longer than customary.

Arabella's heart thudded, and her throat burned.

Old friends, indeed.

A moment later, Susanna leaned up on tiptoe and kissed his cheek, beaming at him. Richard wrapped his arms around her and held her close in a tender embrace.

Arabella's head pounded dully. Stomach souring, she gingerly backed away from the window, praying he would not see her. How mortifying for them all!

She'd been so close to believing a man could change. That *he* had changed. That he truly cared for her. She pressed a hand to her stomach, fearing she might be ill.

But something else rose up as well. Anger, carrying a strong taint of rejection. So be it. It would take an angelic woman to put up with Richard Brockwell, and Arabella was not her.

She recalled Richard saying, *"She has not forgiven me, and I don't blame her."*

Well, apparently, Susanna had finally forgiven him.

Richard had said, *"I will always love her. . . . But I am not in love with her, nor she with me."*

The scene she'd just witnessed belied those words.

Arabella decided she should be relieved to learn the truth now, before it could too deeply hurt her. Before it could alter her plans and ruin her life. She should be grateful for this near escape, for this evidence that solidified her resolve.

But relief and gratitude were not what she felt.

Later that day, Richard found a private moment with his immediate family and said, "I don't have anything for our guests, but I do have small gifts for each of you."

He handed the parcels around: a new novel for Timothy, sheet music for Justina, a decorative sewing box for Rachel, a children's book for Frederick, and for his mother, a small brooch with dark and silver hair woven in a chessboard pattern beneath the glass.

She looked up at him in surprise. "This hair . . . It's not . . . ?"

"Father's, yes. Pickering had saved some. He used to cut Father's hair, you know, as he cuts mine now."

Her large eyes filled with tears, and Richard's chest tightened at the foreign sight. He'd not meant to upset her.

He shifted from foot to foot. "The jeweler said we didn't have enough for anything larger, I'm afraid."

"No, it's . . . it's perfect. Thank you, Richard. I don't know what to say. I have nothing so thoughtful for you."

"I wish I could take all the credit for it, but it was Pickering's idea. I did have it set, but only because he thought of it when I lamented over what to give you."

"I adore it. Thank you. I shall thank him as well. Thank you both."

Richard grew increasingly uncomfortable and patted her hand. "There, there, Mamma. Steady on."

In return, Justina gave him a box of writing supplies—paper, journal, and ink. And Timothy sheepishly handed him a novel—a copy of the same novel Richard had given him.

Richard grinned. "We must think alike."

"Not surprising. We are brothers, after all."

"Yes." Richard met his gaze. "We are."

As the impromptu family party broke up, Timothy asked him, "It seems a little warmer today. What say you to riding together?"

Richard looked at him in surprise. "I would like that."

Half an hour later, the brothers were dressed in riding clothes and mufflers, and mounted two horses.

As they trotted out of the stable yard, Timothy said, "Thank you for coming out. I've missed having a riding companion."

They rode around the church and over the packhorse bridge. Richard observed, "You used to ride with Jane when we were young."

"Yes, but she is happily married now, and so am I. Our days of riding together are in the past."

Turning a corner, Bramble Cottage came into view. Richard murmured, "Speaking of the past . . ."

He'd not intended to be heard, but his brother stilled, looking at him intently. "You know something about Bramble Cottage?"

Richard hedged, pointing into the nearby field. "Our sleigh ended up in the ditch over there, and since Miss Awdry had hurt her foot, we took shelter inside the place. I'd heard it was presently unoccupied and assumed our family still owns it."

"We used to, yes. But why did you assume we owned it? From something in Father's will?"

"No."

"Were you . . . acquainted with the former tenant?"

"Never met her." A pause. "Saw her though."

Timothy studied his face, eyes glinting with questions and specu-
lation. Richard hesitated. Oh, he was tempted. Tempted to knock
the mighty Sir Justin off his pedestal and back to fallen earth. But
at what price? It would be petty and beneath him to disillusion his
brother. No good could come of it after all this time.

Before Richard made up his mind, Timothy said, "I met her."

Surprise flared through Richard. "Did you?"

His brother nodded. "But only a couple of years ago. Mrs.
Haverhill has since moved on to Brighton."

Richard wondered how much Timothy knew. "And what did
you think of her?"

"I did not approve of her. Not at first. But Rachel convinced
me to be more understanding."

Richard raised his eyebrows. "Rachel is acquainted with her
too?"

"Again, they met only recently. It was through her that I learned
some . . . family history of which I was hitherto unaware."

Richard's heart began to pound. "You know?"

"Do you?"

Richard studied his brother's face. "If you are talking about
what I think you are. But Father made me promise years ago never
to tell, so I'd prefer not to speak first."

"I learned that he had bought Bramble Cottage for Mrs. Haverhill. And why."

"Why?" Richard asked, needing to hear him say it.

"Because she was his . . . mistress."

Richard released a long breath, like a balloon under pressure.

Timothy watched him and asked gently, "When did you find
out?"

"Years ago. I was twelve. On my way home from Honeycroft
one day, I saw Father let himself inside Bramble Cottage. It's how
I knew where to find the key. It made me curious, so I looked in
the window. That's when I saw him embrace a woman not our
mother and heard him call her 'my darling Georgiana.'"

Richard didn't repeat the other hurtful words he'd heard him say.

Timothy slowly shook his head. "I am sorry, Richard. What a thing to learn about our father at such an impressionable age."

"I don't imagine you enjoyed the revelation much better at thirty."

"No, but I had Rachel to share it with. What a burden to shoulder yourself. Did you never say anything about what you saw?"

Richard shook his head. "I kept my mouth shut for years, watched him masquerade at home like the honorable squire, when all along I knew his dishonorable secret. My second year of university, however, I became involved with a local woman and was ignominiously 'sent down' from Oxford. Father was more livid than I had ever seen him, berating my character, and saying he was through paying for my education. He also accused me of trifling with a housemaid, but that was not true. At all events, he threatened to cut me off—force me to make my own way in the world and work for a living. I knew the time had come to lay down that ace I'd been saving.

"When I told him what I knew, he asked me to swear on my honor to keep his secret. I said, 'According to you, I haven't any honor. But I am sure we can work out a mutually beneficial arrangement.'"

Timothy raised his chin in sudden realization. "So that's why Father allowed you to live in the townhouse and agreed to fund your London life. I tried to reason with him about the unnecessary expense before he died, but he held firm."

Richard nodded. "I could not get out of Brockwell Court fast enough. Yet his final words to me haunt me still. 'You selfish schemer. You will be the death of me.' Not long after that, he had the apoplexy. 'The stroke of God's hand,' the doctor called it. But I knew it was my fault."

"No, Richard, it was not."

Richard shrugged. "You see now why I've avoided marriage. I've seen firsthand the farce societal unions can be. You know our parents were not happy, though Mamma would never admit it. And once he died, she quickly idealized him, forgetting all his neglect and coolness toward her, the many absences . . . The great Sir Justin, magistrate, so dutifully serving the board of governors for the almshouse, the village council, St. Anne's . . . all the while betraying his family and his marriage vows. What a bag of moonshine. Rubbish, the lot of it. I decided if that's what marriage was, they could keep it."

Richard stared at the silent house. His father's hypocrisy was at least partly why he wrote satire lampooning those who set themselves above others, when they were really sinners like everyone else. He was no saint either, of course, but he didn't pretend to be.

Richard looked at his brother. "But I kept my promise to never tell her. Has Mamma somehow learned of it?"

"Not as far as I know. Certainly not from me. I decided it would only hurt her unnecessarily."

"I agree." Richard would not break his mother's heart if he could help it. Nor break his promise to his father and thereby live up to all the negative things Sir Justin had said about him.

A dark cloud passed overhead, and rain suddenly pelted down. "Come," Timothy said, pulling on one rein. "Let's go home."

Together they galloped back to Brockwell Court. Reaching the stables and seeing no groom about the place, they removed the saddles and rubbed down the horses themselves.

Over the top of the adjoining stall, Timothy said, "I am sorry, Richard. But I'm afraid none of this changes our financial situation. Our decision to sell the townhouse still stands."

The words stole any remaining morsel of hope that Richard could return to his former life. The life he'd thought he wanted. He considered arguing. But how could he argue that he deserved the townhouse, when he knew he deserved nothing? Simply for keeping his father's secret, which would have humiliated his family and himself in the bargain? He had extorted years of free and easy living from that knowledge. It was more than enough.

He nodded to his brother and continued grooming the horse. Inwardly, disappointment gave way to a fear of the unknown. How would he support himself? Where would he live? Could he face himself in the mirror if he simply remained in Brockwell Court, living off his family's largess?

Heaven help him, it would be even more difficult to ask for Arabella's hand without his own home. Timothy had been right when he'd said, "What sort of life could you offer her?" Richard realized anew that he was not good enough for Miss Awdry. Never had been and was certainly less so now.

Even so, he decided he had to try.

Richard led David Murray up the High Street to a small property between the lace maker's and the circulating library. A *For Let* sign stood propped in the window.

Richard asked, "What would you think of a property like this? Would it suit you? Would your printing press fit?"

Murray's eyes shifted to his in surprise.

Richard explained, "I hope you don't mind, but Susanna mentioned your interest in remaining in the area."

"Yes, she assured me you wouldn't mind if I . . . if we . . ."

"I don't mind. I couldn't be happier for you both."

"I am glad to hear it." Murray looked again at the shop, leaning closer to peer through the window. "I wonder how much a place like this rents for here?"

"I don't know." Richard pointed a few doors away. "The property agents are just down the street. We could ask."

Murray hesitated, then shrugged. "There is no point. Whatever it is, I can't afford it. Not now."

Richard studied his friend's profile in concern. "What's wrong? You mentioned the magazine is not as profitable as you'd like. Has something else happened?"

Murray nodded. "I received a letter from my lawyer and financial backer. Apparently, we have declared bankruptcy. And by the time the creditors are through selling off my equipment and furniture, there will be almost nothing left and nothing to go back to."

Shock and sorrow washed over Richard. "You often joked about bankruptcy, but I did not realize things were as bad as all that."

"You're not the only one who hides behind humor."

Richard squeezed his shoulder. "I am sorry, old friend. I wish there was something I could do."

"Don't worry, Richard. I am not asking for help. I know you are facing your own predicament. Only unburdening myself." Murray chuckled, though it was a desolate sound.

Richard inwardly agreed. He faced his own predicament indeed.

CHAPTER

FIFTEEN

When Richard entered the breakfast room early the next morning, Miss Awdry was just leaving. He had seen very little of her the day before, and during shared meals, she seemed to be avoiding eye contact. Was she angry with him for the glib, foolish words he'd spoken in the coach? He certainly regretted those words now and hoped a heartfelt proposal would be better received.

He abandoned his coffee and followed her out.

"Miss Awdry. Arabella. May I speak with you a moment?"

She ran her tongue over her lips, her eyes darting to his and away again. "I am rather busy, Mr. Brockwell. If—"

"Please."

She sighed. "Very well. For a few moments."

He led her into the library, his favorite room in any house.

"I kno . . ." He attempted to clear the nervous lump blocking his throat, then repeated, "I realize I have given you reason to doubt my character and my intentions in the past. But you also said you believe a man can change. I hope you believe I *have* changed. We may have spent less than a fortnight together this Christmas, yet we have known one another for years. I think you are wonderful. And I . . . I love you. Yes, I said I had no intention of marrying, and you have said the same. You, Miss Awdry, have utterly changed my mind. Have I any chance of changing yours?"

She blinked. "Are you sincerely asking me to marry you?"

"Very poorly, no doubt. Nevertheless, I am perfectly sincere."

An incredulous little laugh passed her lips, but she endeavored to compose herself. "Then I am sorry to disappoint you."

The blood in his head began to pound. This was not the reaction he'd hoped for.

She entwined her fingers and spoke formally. "In such cases as this, it is, I believe, the established mode to express gratitude for the offer, so I thank you. However, I cannot accept. I am sorry to occasion pain to anyone and hope it will be of short duration."

Her words stabbed him like a hot cut to his heart. He forced his face to remain impassive and his voice calm. "May I ask why? Is it because of my reputation or past behavior or concerns about my ability to support you?"

Another mirthless laugh. "Such good reasons to choose from! Though I have other provocation—you know I have. I have every reason in the world to doubt your character."

Confusion puckered his brow. "To what do you refer? I am not the man I once was. I thought you admired me, at least a little. And I certainly admire you."

She shrugged, but he could see she didn't believe him.

Richard's mind whirled, searching for a way to convince her, to soften the hard look on her face.

"I know you struggle to believe I could and would be faithful to you. But I would be, Arabella. I promise you."

"How can I believe you? Against the evidence of my own eyes?" She shook her head. "No, I could not bear it. Always wondering. Every late night. Every look at a housemaid . . ."

Indignation flashed. "Miss Awdry. Here you are unjust. I have never dallied with a housemaid in my life."

"Yes, you did. I was here when you were sent home from Oxford. I overheard your father berating you. For years now I have kept your base little secret. One of many, no doubt."

"Thunder and turf. That was years ago! Yes, I flirted with that maid, but that was the end of it. Father found her in my room and assumed the worst. I give you my word, nothing happened."

"I might believe you, if I had not seen you behave in similar fashion more than once since I've been here."

"I have no idea what you are talking about."

She huffed. "Susanna."

"I told you. She and I are old friends. You are the only woman in Ivy Hill, in all of England, I want to marry."

"I don't know what your intentions are toward other women, and I don't care." She held up her palm. "It is none of my business. I had already decided to remain unmarried before I came here, and though I admit to being briefly tempted by you, I will not exchange my independence for a marriage sure to result in betrayal and heartache. I am sorry if that hurts you, but I trust you will recover quickly. In the unlikely event I see you at some London charity event, you will no doubt be with some pretty widow and will have forgotten all about me."

"Impossible."

"That you would attend a charity event? Yes, I know."

"No, I meant—"

"Good-bye, Mr. Brockwell. We are going home early. I am already packed. I realize we were invited to stay through Twelfth Night, but as things are . . . Cyril and his new bride are due home any day, and we want to be there to welcome them. As soon as I can make travel arrangements, I will be moving to London. Better late than never. I doubt our paths will often cross there."

"I doubt it too."

Surprise flickered through her eyes, but he did not explain. She hesitated, then lifted her chin. "Perhaps that is for the best."

Walking in a dejected daze, Richard returned to the empty breakfast room in great need of coffee. The footman came in and handed Richard a letter. He inwardly groaned. What now? Another rejection or another bill from his tailor? The handwriting was not familiar. Richard glanced at the seal, not recognizing the insignia.

He peeled it open, and a slip of paper fell out. He bent to pick it up, expecting an enclosed invoice or past-due notice. Glancing at it, he blinked and looked more closely. It was a bank draft for one hundred pounds, made payable to him and signed by a London banker.

Stunned, he turned his attention to the letter.

It was from the final publisher to whom he'd sent a copy of his book. Richard had all but given up hope of hearing back from the man, let alone of receiving an offer.

We are pleased to publish your novel and consider a second, if our terms are agreeable to you.

It was not as much as an aspiring novelist might hope for. He had heard of authors paid far more for their novels, but he had certainly heard of others paid far less. For an untried author, it really was a very good offer, and more money than he had ever earned in his life. With this much money, he could afford to live in London for another year—in a small pair of rooms, perhaps. and with fewer visits to his tailor, yet it could be done. Perhaps life as he knew it was not over.

For several moments, Richard stared at the letter and bank draft, feeling as though he were trapped in a dream. Fearing any moment he would wake up and both would dissolve in his hands, and all his hopes with them.

Arabella was relieved to return home to Broadmere, but when she broached the subject of London again, her mother groaned.

"Not that again, Arabella."

"Mamma, please. You know how long I have wanted to go to London. Aunt Gen wants me to work with her and has invited me to stay as long as I like."

Lady Lillian looked at her, then sighed, slouching into the sofa without her usual ramrod-straight posture.

"Oh, my beautiful, accomplished daughter. Is your beauty to be all for nothing?"

"Mamma. Remember, 'favour is deceitful and beauty is vain.'"

"Yes, yes. I know. Still . . . I had hoped. Things seemed to be going so well with Richard Brockwell."

Arabella shook her head. "I have turned him down, Mamma."

"He did propose?"

"Yes, though I could not accept him."

"Oh no." Her mother sighed again. "Well. That's that. Now that you have turned down the last Brockwell, and Mr. Bingley has chosen your sister, you may as well go to London. There is no one left for you here."

"Mamma, you should be happy Penelope is engaged."

"I am! I gather Mrs. Bingley hoped Horace would turn his attentions to you. However, I cannot say I am truly sorry. I doubted Penelope would ever receive an offer of marriage, and one from a Bingley? It is more than I could have hoped for. I trust his mother will warm to Penelope in time."

"She will, Mamma. Who could not who truly knows her? Pen will make him an excellent wife and hunting companion. I don't even ride."

"True. Well, I shan't prevent you, but I cannot spare our lady's maid, and naturally you cannot travel alone. So if you are determined, write to your aunt and see what she suggests."

"Very well, I shall. Thank you, Mamma!" Arabella kissed her mother's cheek and hurried up to her room. She quickly wrote to her aunt with the news that her mother had finally relented. Arabella was ready and willing to journey to London at her first opportunity.

Preparing for the outing to come, Richard dressed himself in his most professional coat and tied his cravat into a plain barrel knot. No frippery. No falderals. Pickering watched with silent interest and a touch of concern. Wally, too, made do with a simple warm woolen waistcoat. His dandy days might be over, but it was still winter.

A short while later, Richard wheeled down the drive in the curricle borrowed from his brother, Wally perched happily beside him. As they turned onto Ivy Hill's High Street, Richard glanced at The Bell Inn. It would be so easy to go there and buy passage on a coach that would return him to London.

Instead, he looked away and rode down the hill and eastward into Wishford, his thoughts on Jamie Fleming, David Murray, and the printer Francis Knock.

What sort of system sentenced a vulnerable youth to seven years of bondage to a cruel abuser? Changes were needed. Perhaps it was time he used his writing skills for a higher purpose than lampooning the monarch or other politicians. Richard still had received no reply to the letter he'd written to the organization. If only Murray had not gone bankrupt and his magazine out of business. Richard had waited too long. Was that not the story of his life? He'd squandered the years he'd been given and wasted so many opportunities.

In Wishford, Richard left the horses and curricle in the livery and walked to the print shop.

The burly printer was just returning from his midday meal at the Crown.

"Mr. Knock. I see your *For Sale* notice is still up. No offers?"

"Afraid not."

"I suppose printing is not as profitable as it once was?"

"That's right. Times are hard, especially in a small town like this."

Richard nodded. "As well as in London. In fact, a publisher I know from there has just been forced to declare bankruptcy."

"Poor sap. That's a pity."

"I agree. How long has your place been for sale?"

Knock blew out a breath. "Oh, nigh on two years now." Mr. Knock strode inside and Richard followed him. Wally waited outside, none too patiently.

"So an offer is unlikely at this point?" Richard asked. He sent a subtle smile to Jamie, busy with a broom.

"Yes, but one can still hope. I'd like to sell out. Tired of slaving away for the few coins that come my way. And what thanks do I get? Ink-stained fingers and an ungrateful apprentice eating me out of house and home." He gestured toward Jamie.

The boy did look more hale—thanks more likely to the provisions Mrs. Nettleton had sent back with him than any generosity on Mr. Knock's part.

He kept his tone casual. "What are you asking for the place?"

The man told him, and Richard kept his face serene, even though the amount was far too high.

"Though had I a cash offer on the line, I might consider accepting less," Knock added.

Richard nodded sagely, then grimaced at the shop's peeling paint and sagging ceiling. "The building is not in the best trim."

Knock looked around him, scratching his head, as though this were news to him.

Richard asked, "And where would you live were you to sell?"

"Oh, I don't know. Have not thought that far. Depends on if a new owner wanted to live in or not."

Richard took a deep breath. "I will give you ninety pounds for the equipment, type, and furnishings. Customer lists and accounts. Paper stock. The lot of it."

The man's eyebrows rose to his scalp. "You, Mr. Brockwell? And what would you do with it?"

"Print something, I imagine."

Knock shook his head. "Ninety pounds is not enough."

"Very well." Richard shrugged and turned toward the door.

"Wait. Let's talk this over. Where would I live?"

"You can keep the building. Such as it is. Perhaps you could let out the lower floors and sleep in the rotting garret you consigned your young apprentice to."

"Then where would you set up shop?"

"You leave that to me."

The Ivy Hill property agent had offered him the vacant shop on the High Street on very easy terms.

Knock's brow puckered. "Do you know anything about printing?"

"Very little. Thankfully, I shall have Jamie here to help me." Richard nodded at Jamie but kept his expression detached.

Knock stood possessively beside the lad, chest out. "The apprentice is mine. I've got the papers. It's all legal-like. Seven years."

"You shall not need an apprentice. Unless, what, do you fancy a houseboy or a bootboy? Oh yes, you would like a bootboy, I don't doubt. Even so, you shall not have this one, for he is part of my bargain. Take it or leave it."

Lifting a pugnacious chin, Knock said, "You can't do that. I have a contract. In my name."

Jamie looked as miserable as a boy could, but Richard endeavored to keep his cards close to his chest.

"Well, I'm sure we can find a magistrate to make the necessary alterations. My brother is one of the local JPs, and both Lord

Winspear and Mr. Bingley are personal friends. But if you'd rather have the apprentice than an offer of ready cash, then . . ."

Again Richard turned to go, trying not to succumb to Jamie's forlorn expression.

The printer called, "I didn't say that. Don't be hasty. I have to think."

"I'll give you one minute." Richard sighed theatrically, gazing around the shoddy shop. "Already I am second-guessing the idea of sinking my money into such a failing enterprise."

"I'll take it. Cash on the barrelhead."

"Oh, very well." Richard huffed and handed over several bank-notes.

At that moment, a familiar older woman threw back the door, which slammed against the wall, startling them all. She strode into the shop, her heels thumping like gunshots, her sharp gaze cutting from Richard to the boy and then settling on the man in the stained apron.

"Mr. Knock?"

"Yes, madam. How may I help you?"

"I am Miss Arbuthnot, directress of the St. George Orphan Refuge. I have received a letter informing me that you are not at all a suitable master and have abused the privilege."

"Says who?"

"As I said, I received a letter from a concerned citizen and have spent the last hour interviewing your neighbors and the local physician."

"I've read the contract," Knock insisted. "There's no stipulation for mollycoddling the lad."

"But there are stipulations for proper care, accommodation, and wholesome meals. None of which you apparently provide."

"He's got a roof over his head."

Miss Arbuthnot pulled out the letter and read, "'. . . a roof riddled with holes and a pallet wet and rotting. And if the boy is given more than a few scraps of food a day, I should be very much surprised. He is given more straps than scraps.'"

Richard thought it quite poetic, but Knock frowned.

"Whoever wrote that exaggerates. I've fed him while he's here. Trained him. That's worth a lot."

"And you were paid an apprenticeship fee for caring for and training the boy. You have not held up your end of the bargain, so the boy will not spend another night here. I intend to void the contract."

"You can't do that."

"I can, actually." She glanced at Richard. "Assuming we can get a local magistrate to approve the change?"

"That can definitely be arranged," Richard replied.

Knock crossed his beefy arms. "Well, there's nothing in the contract about paying back the fee should the contract be canceled."

The woman's nostrils flared. "An oversight I plan to address as soon as possible. We will also begin verifying the character and reputation of potential masters in the future to ensure such mistreatment does not happen again."

A quarter of an hour later, details discussed and business concluded, Richard opened the door for Miss Arbuthnot and followed her outside.

"We had better go and see Sir Timothy straightaway," she said. "Before that man takes it into his head to accuse Jamie of absconding."

"I agree."

Extracting his small purse from his pocket, Richard said, "If you are in earnest about making changes to your charity, allow me to be the first to make a contribution."

She sent him a frosty look, her mouth a stern line. "*If?* Do I look like the sort of woman who does not stand by her word?"

"Far from it." Removing a banknote, he said, "My last ten pounds. All I have left after putting this scoundrel out of business."

She accepted it, eyes glinting. "Thank you. I shall put it to good use. But, if I may ask, don't you need this for yourself . . . or for your favorite coffeehouse and bookshop?"

Ah, so she had recognized him from London.

He smiled. "Between us, I've had some good news. A publisher has given me a tidy sum for my novel, and is interested in my second one too, which I am revising presently."

"Congratulations."

"Thank you, madam. You are the first to know."

She inclined her head. "I am honored." Looking back toward the printer's, she said, "After we call on Sir Timothy, I suppose I ought to go and visit my sister and nieces. The Awdrys. I imagine you are acquainted with them?"

"Why yes, I am. In fact, they spent the Christmas holidays with us at Brockwell Court, but they've just gone home to Broadmere." Realization struck. "Ah! You must be the Aunt Gen Miss Arabella speaks of so highly."

She nodded, confirming dryly, "Genevieve Arbuthnot, her mother's bluestocking sister."

Richard chewed his lip, then added, "When you see Miss Arabella, please tell her I harbor no resentment and wish her all the best for her future."

Miss Arbuthnot looked at him with keen interest, her dark eyes alight and much too knowing.

Jamie came outside, a threadbare valise in hand and fear in his expression. Wally came over to greet him, but the boy was too overcome to acknowledge the besotted creature.

"Am I to start all over with someone else, sir?" he asked. "Or am I on my own now?"

Richard squeezed the boy's shoulder. "We'll find a new situation for you, a far better one. Don't worry. In the meantime, what do you say to a few more nights in Brockwell Court? Best food for miles."

"May I visit the servants' hall again?"

"Of course! Mrs. Nettleton will be happy to see you, as will Mrs. Dean and Pickering."

Jamie smiled with relief and bent to pet Wally. "Thank you, sir. It will be like Christmas all over again!"

Arabella bundled up and walked outside alone, breathing in the brisk January air and the stillness of a winter's day. Cyril and his new wife had arrived home last night, and Arabella's ears needed a respite from the constant chatter and incessant laughter. She *was* happy for her brother and his bride, and for Penelope and Horace, but her own heart felt heavy. She needed solitude to think. To pray.

The sound of horse hooves and jingling tack caught her ear, and she turned and saw a post chaise and four horses approach. They were not expecting visitors. Arabella watched, her curiosity doubling when the vehicle turned up Broadmere's drive.

Arabella glimpsed her aunt's stern face framed in the window, and surprise and eagerness pulsed through her.

She hurried over to greet her. "Aunt Gen! What are you doing here?"

"Good day, Arabella." The older woman accepted the groom's hand and stepped down, smoothing the skirt of her plain carriage dress.

Confused, Arabella said, "My letter could not have reached you yet. I just wrote to you yesterday, and here you are!"

"I did not receive your letter. I am here because of a different one." While the Broadmere groom directed the chaise to the carriage house, her aunt explained, "I received a letter about an apprentice our charity had sent to Wishford. A sweet-natured lad named Jamie."

"Jamie Fleming? Yes, I met him."

Her aunt nodded. "I met him myself while he lived in the orphan refuge. A good boy. But apparently the master is unsuitable."

"I agree."

Her aunt waved a gloved hand. "Well. More about that later. What did you write to me about?"

"To let you know that I begged Mamma to let me go to London, and she has finally relented. However, she cannot spare the lady's maid we share, and I cannot travel alone. But now you are here, I can travel back with you. No one could object to that!"

Genevieve watched her closely.

When her aunt did not immediately reply, Arabella found her voice rising in pitch. "You said you wanted me to help you, that I was welcome to stay with you in London."

"I did. You are," her aunt soothed, patting her hand. "My dear, I would so enjoy your company and have no doubt you would be a great asset to the charity. There is only one thing I would like better. Your happiness."

"I will be happy."

"Are you sure this is what you want?"

"It is."

Her aunt hesitated a moment longer, then said, "Very well. Then you had better start packing." The older woman looked up at the house and took a fortifying breath. "And I suppose I ought to visit my ninny-headed sister while I am here. Shall we go in before we freeze to death?"

Miss Arbuthnot spent the evening with her sister, older niece, nephew, and his wife, while Arabella and the lady's maid packed a trunk for London.

In the morning, when all was prepared, Arabella kissed her family, and together, she and her aunt rode away from Broadmere in the post chaise.

After a time of companionable silence, her aunt began, "I told you yesterday that I received a letter about the apprentice. But I did not tell you everything."

"Oh?"

The older woman nodded. "The letter I received was well written. Strident, yet effective. And as my board of governors had sent the boy into the brute's hands, I drove there to witness the mistreatment for myself. Unfortunately, I was too late."

"Too late? Oh no! Tell me Jamie was not seriously injured, or worse!"

"He has been put out of his misery."

"No!"

Her aunt frowned. "You needn't look so shocked, Arabella. I only meant that another man has released Jamie from his oppressor."

Arabella released a sigh of relief. "Oh, good."

Aunt Gen looked at her, wiry eyebrows high. "Have you not guessed who?"

Arabella shook her head.

Genevieve Arbuthnot sighed. "You are your mother's daughter. Silly creature. It was Richard Brockwell who wrote to me. I understand your families are well acquainted. He criticized the governors for not investigating the suitability of situations before subjecting a young person to an abusive man's power. I did not like being reproved, nor being summoned, but he was right. It is an oversight in our procedures that we must address. I am grateful to him for bringing the situation to my attention."

"I am glad he did so. I am sorry I did not think to do so myself."

"He also donated his last ten pounds to the St. George Orphan Refuge."

Arabella felt her brows rise. "Richard Brockwell? Are we talking about *my* Richard Brockwell?"

"Is he yours? I had not realized."

Arabella's face instantly flamed. "Of course not, I simply doubted it could be Richard Brockwell from Ivy Hill. For the man I know would never do such a thing."

"Then the man you know has changed."

Had he? Was it possible? Arabella shook her head. "Last I heard, Richard Brockwell planned to return to London to continue his self-indulgent life as a gentleman of leisure."

The older woman shook her head. "The Brockwells are selling the London townhouse. I overheard as much when I called on Sir Timothy about the apprenticeship agreement."

Compassion squeezed Arabella's heart. "That will be a disappointment to Richard. I wonder how and where he will live, as he has no income of his own."

"Well, thankfully, his first novel will soon be published, and he is currently revising a second."

Arabella turned to stare at her. "Really?"

"Yes."

Arabella absorbed the surprising news and for several minutes gazed idly out at the passing countryside without actually seeing anything. Suddenly she recognized the landscape and frowned.

"Aunt Gen, your driver has made a mistake and turned toward Ivy Hill. We should have continued south to Salisbury and taken the London Road from there."

"It is no mistake. I told him to drive this way."

"Why?"

"There is something I want you to see."

"I have already seen Ivy Hill. I just spent almost a fortnight there."

"I know, yet I think something there will interest you. It certainly interested me."

"Oh?"

She nodded. "Mr. Brockwell used the money he received for his first novel to buy printing equipment for his friend. Business partners, he says, but I saw Mr. Murray's name in the *Gazette*. He has declared bankruptcy, so I doubt he contributed much capital to the enterprise. Also, Mr. Brockwell and I convinced Sir Timothy to transfer the apprentice's term to Mr. Murray, who seems an excellent man. He plans to settle in Ivy Hill. I have heard he is soon to be engaged to a local woman—an old friend of Richard's apparently. The way I see it, Mr. Brockwell has rescued the boy and his friends in the bargain."

Arabella blinked, taking it all in, her mind shifting. What she thought she knew about Richard Brockwell tilted and spun like a globe on its axis. "Goodness . . ." she breathed. "I had no idea."

Aunt Gen patted her hand. "Well, my dear. A belated Christmas gift, I'd say."

Arabella nodded but silently thought, *More like a Christmas miracle.*

As the carriage rattled up the rise and along the Ivy Hill High Street, Arabella saw the carter's wagon heavily loaded with crates and several pieces of furniture. A few workmen were levering and pushing a printing press through the doorway, the frame of which had been removed to allow the contraption to pass.

Among the workmen, she was startled to recognize Richard Brockwell, in a plain grey coat, straining and sweating with the rest. His dark hair had been tousled by the wind, perspiration glistened on his aristocratic features, and a black smear streaked one cheekbone. He had never looked more handsome.

He said something to Mr. Murray beside him, and then smiled reassurance at the young apprentice, who carried a smaller load past them.

"They are moving the print shop here?" Arabella asked.

Aunt Gen nodded. "Did I not say you would find it interesting?"

"You were right. May I step out for a few minutes to wish them well?"

"Yes, if you'd like." She knocked on the roof of the carriage with her stick, and the driver brought the equipage to a halt. The groom hopped down and helped Arabella alight.

She saw Mr. Murray lean near the lovely young widow, Susanna, and say something in her ear. She smiled softly in return and slipped her hand into his. This was the nurserymaid Arabella had seen with Richard and had assumed the two were romantically involved. She'd assumed wrong. Susanna was clearly in love with his friend. How had she not seen it?

Richard noticed Arabella and stilled. For a moment their gazes met and held across the distance. Then he walked toward her, wiping his hands on a handkerchief as he came.

"Miss Awdry. I assumed you and your aunt would be well on your way to London by now."

"One should never assume, Mr. Brockwell, as I have learned to my deep regret."

He looked at her in bemusement and made no reply.

Nervous, she repeated the same foolish question to him. "You are setting up a print shop here?"

He looked over his shoulder. "Yes. The building in Wishford was falling to ruin, but more than that, I knew Murray had reason to want to be here in Ivy Hill."

"And is that reason's name Susanna?"

He looked back at her. "It's not my place to say, yet I do predict Rachel will soon have to find a new nurserymaid."

Arabella tilted her head to the side. "How do you feel about that?"

"I could not be happier for them and am pleased to have had a hand in bringing two dear friends together. He is an excellent man, not a useless dandy like me."

She shook her head. "Hardly useless. I hope you don't mind— Aunt Gen told me about your letter to her and about the publishing offer. I am so happy for you."

"Thank you. It is a relief, I admit."

"And of all the things you might have done with the proceeds, you chose to set up your friend in business?"

Richard tugged at his shirt collar. "Don't make me out to be a saint, Miss Awdry—for I am not. I am by nature a selfish creature and always shall be, though I strive against it. Mr. Murray and I are business partners."

She decided not to mention what she knew about his friend's financial situation.

He changed the subject. "And you, Miss Awdry? On your way to London to devote yourself to good works?"

He said it sincerely, without derision, which gave her pause. She nodded. "You know I want to make a difference in this world. That has not changed. I want my life to count for something."

He looked at her, as serious as she'd ever seen him. "Your life already counts, Arabella Awdry, whether you ever go to London or not. You are valuable and significant, just as you are. Your family loves you, and I . . . I would be remiss not to remind you of all the good you've done even in the brief time you were here—playing music at the charity school, assembling Christmas baskets for poor families, visiting the elderly at the almshouse, and bringing joy by caroling with your lovely voice, your lovely . . . everything." He cleared his throat.

Arabella looked down, face heating anew.

The toes of his shoes neared her hem. His voice low, he added, "And let us not forget your life-changing impact on a certain prodigal who values you above all others."

Arabella glanced shyly up at him. "Oh, I think God was already working in that prodigal's life. I may have just . . . helped Him along."

The two shared fond smiles. Richard swallowed, then said, "Well, I won't try to stop your going, much as I'm tempted. I hope you find everything you seek in London."

Behind them the chaise door opened, and a voice called, "Arabella, it's time we were on the road."

She then turned back to Richard. "I have to go."

He gave her a lopsided grin. "Visit my favorite bookseller for me."

"I shall." She looked into his eyes for a long moment, then resolutely turned away.

Twelfth Night, or the eve of Epiphany, marked the coming of the magi. This year, instead of the usual masquerade ball, costumes, and revelry, the Brockwells' Twelfth Night party became more of a celebration of not one but two engagements: Horace Bingley and Penelope, and Justina and Nicholas Ashford.

Though disappointed that Richard was still unattached, Lady Barbara relinquished her objections to Mr. Ashford and had given her blessing for him and Justina to wed. The couple was delighted.

Yet the most jubilant bride-to-be was Penelope Awdry. Rachel had never seen her look happier or more radiant, blushing and smiling and remaining near Mr. Bingley's side. Rachel was pleased for her and Horace both and only sorry Arabella was not there to celebrate their engagement.

Rachel expanded the happy occasion by inviting several other friends to join them: Jane and Gabriel Locke and their son, Jack Avi, Joseph and Mercy Kingsley and her aunt Matilda, the vicar, Mr. Paley and his family, among others, as well as Jamie Fleming. Rachel also invited Susanna Evans and her family, but Susanna had not felt comfortable accepting. Instead, David Murray was spending the evening at Honeycroft with them.

For the party, Rachel and Mrs. Nettleton had planned a buffet supper with many desserts: jellies, mince pies, marzipan, and an elaborate Twelfth Night cake from Craddock's Bakery, with colored icing and decorative gilded paper trimmings.

They enjoyed music by local musicians along with tea, punch, and cider to add to the general cheer. The youngest among them—the vicar's sons, Jack Avi, and Jamie Fleming—bobbed for apples and played hunt the slipper. They ate too many sweets and sneaked treats to Wally and Lady Barbara's pug, who had become fast friends.

The games Rachel had planned for the adults did not transpire. Friendly conversation, hearty congratulations, laughter, and good-natured teasing filled the hours instead.

Rachel had rarely seen her mother-in-law so happy. Lady Barbara wore her new brooch, held her grandson in her arms, and stood between her children—all except one soon to be married.

"Richard, my dear boy. You will be next. I know it!" She kissed him, Justina, and Timothy in turn, beaming from one to the other. In response, little Frederick gave his grandmamma a wet, sloppy kiss of his own.

At one point in the evening, Lady Barbara took Richard, Timothy, and Rachel aside and said, "I have been thinking. You are welcome to live here, Richard. I hope that goes without saying. But I thought we might buy you a small house nearby—with Timothy's approval, of course. Apparently, one called Bramble Cottage is for sale. Perhaps with some alteration it might be made commodious enough for a soon-to-be published author?"

Sir Timothy's gaze flashed to Richard, then to Rachel—the three of them who knew the history of Bramble Cottage. Timothy cleared his throat. "A . . . em . . . cottage like that one, may not suit, Mamma. It would be rather humble compared to the townhouse or Brockwell Court."

Richard smiled reassuringly from person to person. "Not too humble for me. Thank you, Mamma. A cottage sounds perfect. I can write anywhere."

Rachel and Timothy shared a look of surprise. "Well," Timothy said. "Good. We can discuss the details later."

Around ten that night, families with children began saying their farewells, and by eleven, all but the houseguests had departed, everyone determined to get home in time to take down their own decorations before midnight.

In Brockwell Court, the family, servants, and guests worked together, hurrying around the house and taking down all the decorations before the last stroke of twelve, to avoid bad luck in the coming year. Rachel found it rather humorous to see well-dressed ladies and gentlemen pulling down greenery and tossing holly berries at one another, laughing and teasing.

"You missed a branch. Pick it up! Do you want a goblin to come inside?"

It wasn't that they put much stock in luck, but it *was* tradition. And even if the people of Ivy Hill didn't believe in bad luck or goblins, they believed in tradition.

All the pine, holly, and ivy, all the yew, rosemary, and bay were carried out and tossed onto a large bonfire behind the house. And what aromatic smoke rose from it!

Richard looked around him. Everyone else, it seemed, had gone out to the bonfire or to their beds. He stood alone in the drawing room, looking again at every window, chandelier, and mantel to make sure nothing was left. His gaze landed on the garland around his father's portrait, surprised his mother had missed it. He carried over a ladder-back chair, climbed up, and took down the faded roses. He lingered a moment, studying his father's face, so like his own. Looking his father in the eye, he whispered, "I forgive you, Papa. And I hope you forgave me."

The clock began to chime.

Before the last stroke of midnight, Richard jogged outside, tossing the garland onto the bonfire and the past with it. There, he joined the others gathered around, talking and laughing and relishing the warmth of flames, friends, and family.

Christmas in Ivy Hill was coming to a close. He could go home to London now, if he wanted to. But he did not. He was home already.

EPILOGUE

Arabella took up residence in her aunt's guest room and in her aunt's London life. While other young women of her age and background attended the opera or the few off-season balls or routs, Arabella attended charity concerts at the Foundling Hospital and benefits for the British and Foreign Bible Society and the Ladies Royal Benevolent Society, which hosted sermons at St. James's to raise funds for its work among poor, sick females. She quickly became involved in her aunt's work, volunteering her time, donating her own money, and being richly rewarded in return. At an event for the Magdalen Hospital, Arabella was invited to play the harp and afterward met William Wilberforce and one of the princesses.

The weeks, then months passed in satisfying effort. If not attending an event or committee meeting of an evening, she and Aunt Gen and some of her friends gathered to knit booties and tiny blankets to supply one of several lying-in charities. The hours spent over tea, needlework, and good-natured teasing reminded her of the Ladies Tea and Knitting Society meeting she had visited in Ivy Hill.

Arabella's days were devoted to raising money, promoting subscriptions, writing letters of appeal, and spending time in the St. George Orphan Refuge, inspecting the premises with the matron, helping her aunt engage new staff and instructors when needed, and—Arabella's favorite—talking with the children about their histories and hopes and the skills they were learning.

One afternoon, among the correspondence related to their various charitable endeavors, Arabella received a letter postmarked *Ivy Hill, Wilts.* Her heart gave a little foolish leap, as it always did when thinking of Ivy Hill. It was not from Richard Brockwell, of course. Single gentlemen did not write to single ladies unless they were engaged or had her family's permission. The letter was from Mercy Kingsley, mistress of the Fairmont Boarding & Day School.

> *My dear Miss Awdry,*
>
> *I trust you are enjoying life in London. I wanted to thank you again for playing the harp so beautifully for the children at Christmas and allowing some of the older students to try their hand at the instrument. They still speak of you and of the experience often and fondly! I don't want to discourage or dissuade you from your present course if you are content, but if you should ever decide to return to our area, I would be pleased to offer you a situation teaching music here at the Fairmont charity school. . . .*

Arabella stared at the letter, and for a moment the words blurred before her eyes as she imagined what it would be like to live in Ivy Hill and teach in the school. Her mother would decry a paid position as beneath her, but she might volunteer instead.

Naturally, she could not think of Ivy Hill without thinking of Richard. She knew, from a letter Justina had sent, that he had taken up residence in Bramble Cottage. She could imagine him there in that snug abode, writing away on his next book. Could see so clearly his handsome face, his teasing, admiring eyes. Then she imagined the two of them sitting in church together and afterward walking arm in arm down the street. . . .

Coming into the room, Aunt Gen paused, staring down at her. "What has you smiling?"

"Oh. Only a letter from Ivy Hill."

One wiry brow rose. "Ivy Hill?"

Arabella refolded the note. "From Mrs. Kingsley, the school-mistress."

"Humph. Thought it might be from Mr. Brockwell." Aunt Gen dropped a folded publication on the desk. "This will have to tide you over instead."

Her aunt had taken to scanning all the various newspapers and magazines she read and giving anything about or by Richard Brockwell to Arabella. Today appeared another article he had written about the state of apprentices in the country. She was relieved to see he had credited the St. George Orphan Refuge with changing their procedures for approving masters and called on other organizations to do likewise.

Later that spring, Arabella began helping her aunt plan an anniversary dinner for the orphan refuge. Tireless in her efforts, Arabella organized a dinner, benefit concert, and ball to rival any other in the metropolis. She met with the tavern owners about the menu, engaged performers, and promoted the event, writing articles for the newspapers and invitations to dignitaries and neighbors alike.

The project consumed several months and much of Arabella's energies. Thankfully, she liked being busy. Her aunt grumbled about the pace Arabella set, but she could see the older woman was grateful for her efforts.

Finally, the big day came and went according to plan: the dinner delicious, the concert inspiring, the ball delightful.

Aunt Genevieve seemed thoroughly pleased. "The event was a resounding success. Never before have we brought in so much money in one evening. You have done well, my dear. I am so proud of you."

"Thank you." Arabella smiled. She felt satisfied at a job well done, yet also sensed a catch in her spirit. Something was missing. She ought to feel exultant, but a dull hollowness lingered beneath her breastbone. She realized what it was, but keeping busy had held it at bay. Now that the all-consuming event was over, she could no longer refrain from naming the ache for what she knew it to be.

Loneliness.

That autumn, Aunt Gen came in and laid another publication on the desk. This time, however, the circled paragraph was not an article about the plight of apprentices, orphans, or the like. It was a review of Richard's first book. Arabella held her breath and read, then released a sigh of relief. "'Interesting characters. Clever and amusing. Though the ending is wanting, overall a well-written first novel.'" Arabella looked up. "This is quite positive for the *Quarterly Review*."

"I agree."

A few weeks later, Aunt Gen brought in another newspaper with an advertisement circled in ink. "Hatchards Booksellers is announcing the arrival of Mr. Brockwell's novel. Shall we go and buy a copy?"

Arabella's pulse quickened at the thought. Although not the same as seeing Richard again, reading his novel would give her insight into the man and be the next best thing. Keeping her tone as placid as possible, she said, "If you would like, I have no objection."

Her aunt turned to stare at her. "Are you not interested?"

"Well, I own I am curious. He is a friend, after all."

"Right. A friend."

The next day they hailed a hackney coach to take them to 187 Piccadilly, the bookshop next to Fortnum & Mason—grocer, tea dealer, and spice importer.

Two bays of mullioned windows flanked the shop's center doorway. Above these were painted the words

HATCHARDS BOOKSELLERS TO THE KING.
ESTABLISHED 1797.

Arabella paused at the display in the first bow window. Her aunt came and stood beside her. There it was. Richard's first published novel in the window of his favorite bookseller. He should be standing here, seeing this. She wished she were an artist and could capture the sight for him.

Her aunt said, "Shall we go in and buy a copy, or stand out here gawping at it all day?"

Accustomed to her aunt's brusque humor by now, Arabella grinned like a little girl with a present to unwrap. "Let's go in."

That night, Arabella climbed into bed with the new novel, candle lamp on the side table nearby. As she read the lines, she could hear Richard's voice in her ear. She recognized his wry humor and quick wit, yes, but also discovered a deeper, sensitive nature. Arabella pressed a hand to her beating heart. The book itself was not suggestive or overly sensual, yet there was something strangely intimate about reading Richard Brockwell's words in her own bed. As she read about the novel's hero, it was Richard Brockwell she saw, his tall figure, handsome face, and beguiling mouth . . .

She pressed her eyes closed with a groan. *Oh, you romantic fool*, she chastised herself. If Aunt Gen could guess her thoughts, she'd call her ninny-headed for sure.

Richard sat at a small desk in Bramble Cottage, scratching away with quill and ink. The cottage was perfect for writing. Quiet, peaceful, lovely . . . though admittedly lonely. Now and again Murray stopped by with Peter and Hannah. Or Mrs. Reeves would come by with a pot of honey or plate of biscuits. Pickering had remained at Brockwell Court. Their old butler Carville had finally retired, and Timothy offered the position to Pickering. Richard didn't blame his former valet for not wanting to live in this humble cottage with him alone, not when Mrs. Dean lived in the far finer Brockwell Court. But Richard actually missed the crusty man's company.

With Rachel's help, he had instead engaged Mrs. Mullins to work a few hours every morning, tidying up, cooking a pot of stew, or putting on clean sheets back from the laundress, while one of her sons chopped wood or scythed the lawn, or whatever else needed doing out of doors. Richard dressed and shaved himself, laid his own fires, made his own coffee, and washed up his own dishes, which were few indeed. He dined at Brockwell Court a few evenings a week and enjoyed spending time with his nephew and sister. And he regularly went riding with his brother.

He missed Wally too. With Murray's permission, he had given the dog to Jamie Fleming, or rather Wally had chosen for himself a young new master, always seeking the boy out, whining when called away from his side. Richard had given in, and though he missed the scruffy animal's presence, he was glad he could still visit both the boy and his dog in the nearby High Street whenever he wished.

At the thought, he put on his greatcoat and gloves and went out for his almost daily walk. The early December days were growing cold already, and he increased his pace to warm up. He strode into the village and down the High Street. He noted with satisfaction a display of Reeves honey in the window of Prater's Universal Stores and Post Office and while there, posted a letter to his publisher.

On the way back, he stopped at the print shop to see how Murray and Jamie were getting on. The two worked together companionably on an order of calling cards and sheets of new music for the upcoming Christmas season. Both boy and dog came forward eagerly to greet him, Wally's tail wagging as he nudged Richard's shin with his head, begging to be petted. Wally accepted Richard's affection but then returned to his new master's side. Seeing Jamie's happiness and contentment with his new life was all the gratitude Richard needed.

He continued his stroll, waving to neighbors, shopkeepers, and farmers passing by in their wagons as he went. Walks, he'd found, never failed to stir his mind and spark his imagination.

He returned to Bramble Cottage, eager to write down a new idea for a scene that had stymied him all morning. He took his place at the desk, filled his quill with ink, and began scratching away again. Yes, yes . . . the solution he'd been hoping for presented itself at last. *Thank you, Lord.*

A knock sounded at the door. Richard kept writing.

Bang, bang. Another knock, more persistent this time. With a groan, Richard set down his quill and pushed back his chair. Probably Mrs. Snyder, or perhaps Peter Evans come to chat. Suppressing a sigh, he reminded himself that a visit from a neighbor was not an unwelcome interruption.

He opened the door and stilled.

Definitely not an unwelcome visitor.

There stood Arabella Awdry, even more beautiful than he remembered.

"Miss Awdry. What a surprise."

He glanced behind her and saw the waiting chaise, her aunt visible in its open doorway.

"We are on our way to Broadmere," Arabella began, "but I wanted to stop and congratulate you."

"Oh?"

"I have been following your articles with interest, as well as reviews for your new book. Aunt Gen and I bought a copy at Hatchards. I recently finished it and thought it excellent. Well done."

"Thank you." He took a steadying breath. "And you? How goes life in London? Fruitful?"

"Yes, I think so."

He nodded toward the chaise. "You and your aunt are visiting for the upcoming holidays, I imagine?"

"Yes. That is . . . she will return to London afterward. I plan to stay. Mrs. Kingsley has asked me to teach music in her school, and I have agreed."

He felt his brows rise, and his hopes. "I am surprised but happy to hear it."

She nodded. "I enjoyed my time in London, working beside my aunt. Even so, I missed my family. And I missed . . . you. I now realize I don't have to live in London to do something worthwhile with my life. I can serve God and my fellow man wherever I am."

Richard swallowed, then said, "Perhaps even here, with me?"

She nodded, her eyes shining. "Yes."

Arabella loosened the gathered opening of her reticule. "I know it's early for decorations, but I bought this from an old woman at a coaching inn." She extracted a small branch of mistletoe complete with white berries. "I was sorry we never had a chance to use your kissing bough last Christmas."

His eyes widened, and joy shot through him. "We can remedy that now."

She raised it over their heads, and he smiled into her eyes, then lowered his gaze to her mouth. Slowly, he leaned near, fingers cupping her cheek, his other arm encircling her waist. He pressed his lips softly and sweetly to hers, then kissed her again more deeply.

"All right, you two," Mrs. Arbuthnot called from the waiting chaise. "I'm not getting any younger or warmer sitting out here. Your mother will wonder what became of us. Are you ready to go, or have you had a change of heart?"

Arabella looked at her aunt, then turned back to Richard, smiling up into his face. "Yes, I have had a change of heart. That is it exactly."

Author's Note

I hope you enjoyed spending Christmastime in Ivy Hill, whether this was your first visit to the village, or you are a returning friend who's read the entire TALES FROM IVY HILL series.

I had so much fun writing this novella and researching Christmas traditions in nineteenth-century England. If you want to add a British flair to your own modern celebration, you might buy (or make) mince tarts, Christmas pudding, or fruit cake; place Christmas "crackers" (pull-apart gift tubes) on your table and wear the included paper crowns; refer to Father Christmas instead of Santa; watch the monarch's annual Christmas broadcast; and wish everyone a hearty "Happy Christmas."

Now, I'd like to express my appreciation to a few special people.

Thank you and love to my first reader, Cari Weber. Also to Anna Paulson for her input and help with the move all game scene. As always, thank you to my editors, Karen Schurrer, Kate Deppe, and Raela Schoenherr, and to everyone at Bethany House Publishers who designs, reviews, edits, proofreads, and promotes my books. Fond affection also goes to author Michelle Griep and agent Wendy Lawton for their critiques, prayers, and friendship.

Gratitude and admiration to author Jane Austen, who never

ceases to inspire me. Keen readers may have noticed a few nods to her novels *Emma* and *Pride and Prejudice* within these pages.

Finally, I want to thank every store and library that carries my books and every one of you who reads them. I would not want to do this without you.

Happy Christmas!

Honeycroft Honey-Spice Biscuits (Cookies)

½ cup	butter (softened)
⅔ cup	granulated sugar
2 tablespoons	honey
1	egg yolk
1¼ cups	all-purpose flour
1 teaspoon	cinnamon
¼ teaspoon	ground cloves
¼ teaspoon	ground ginger
1 teaspoon	baking powder
½ teaspoon	fine salt
¼ cup	granulated sugar or colored sugar (e.g., red) for a festive touch
½ teaspoon	cinnamon

In a large bowl, cream the butter and sugar. Add honey and egg yolk. Mix till smooth.

In a medium bowl, whisk the flour, cinnamon, cloves, ginger, baking powder, and salt together and add to wet mixture. Stir and knead until dough holds together. Form into walnut-sized balls.

In a small bowl, mix the cinnamon and sugar.

Roll the dough balls in the cinnamon-sugar mixture.

Place on cookie sheet lined with parchment paper. Bake for 10–11 minutes at 350° F, until tops begin to crack. Do not overbake. Transfer to wire rack to cool.

Makes approximately twenty cookies.

Julie Klassen loves all things Jane—*Jane Eyre* and Jane Austen. Her books have sold over a million copies, and she is a three-time recipient of the Christy Award for Historical Romance. *The Secret of Pembrooke Park* was honored with the Minnesota Book Award for Genre Fiction. Julie has also won the Midwest Book Award and Christian Retailing's BEST Award, and has been a finalist in the RITA and Carol Awards. A graduate of the University of Illinois, Julie worked in publishing for sixteen years and now writes full-time. Julie and her husband have two sons and live in a suburb of St. Paul, Minnesota. For more information, you can follow her on Facebook or visit www.julieklassen.com.

Sign Up for Julie's Newsletter

Keep up to date with Julie's news on book releases and events by signing up for her email list at julieklassen.com.

More from Julie Klassen

Visit the idyllic English village of Ivy Hill, where friendships thrive, romance blossoms, and mysteries await. As the villagers of Ivy Hill search for answers about the past and hope for the future, might they find love along the way?

TALES FROM IVY HILL: *The Innkeeper of Ivy Hill, The Ladies of Ivy Cottage, The Bride of Ivy Green*

You May Also Like . . .

While Benjamin investigates a mysterious death, evidence takes him to a remote island on the Thames. There, Isabelle is trapped by fear and has a recurring dream about a man's death. Or is it a memory? When a murder brings everyone under suspicion, and the search for truth brings secrets to light, she realizes her island sanctuary will never be the same.

The Bridge to Belle Island by Julie Klassen
julieklassen.com

Years of hard work enabled Douglas Shaw to escape a life of desperate poverty—and now he's determined to marry into high society to prevent reliving his old circumstances. But when Alice McNeil, an unconventional telegrapher at his firm, raises the ire of a vindictive co-worker, he must choose between rescuing her reputation and the future he's always planned.

Line by Line by Jennifer Delamere, Love along the Wires #1
jenniferdelamere.com

In the midst of the Great War, Margot De Wilde spends her days deciphering intercepted messages. But after a sudden loss, her world is turned upside down. Lieutenant Drake Elton returns wounded from the field, followed by a destructive enemy. Immediately smitten with Margot, how can Drake convince a girl who lives entirely in her mind that sometimes life's answers lie in the heart?

The Number of Love by Roseanna M. White, The Codebreakers #1
roseannamwhite.com

More from Bethany House

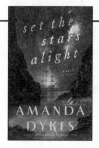

Reeling from the loss of her parents, Lucie Clairmont discovers an artifact under the floorboards of their London flat, leading her to an old seaside estate. Aided by her childhood friend Dashel, a renowned forensic astronomer, they start to unravel a history of heartbreak, sacrifice, and love begun 200 years prior—one that may offer the healing each seeks.

Set the Stars Alight by Amanda Dykes
amandadykes.com

When a strange man appears to be stealing horses at the neighboring estate, Bianca Snowley jumps to their rescue. And when she discovers he's the new owner, she can't help but be intrigued—but romance is unfeasible when he proposes they help secure spouses for each other. Will they see everything they've wanted has been there all along before it's too late?

Vying for the Viscount by Kristi Ann Hunter
Hearts on the Heath
kristiannhunter.com

Determined to uphold her father's legacy, newly graduated Nora Shipley joins an entomology research expedition to India to prove herself in the field. In this spellbinding new land, Nora is faced with impossible choices—between saving a young Indian girl and saving her career, and between what she's always thought she wanted and the man she's come to love.

A Mosaic of Wings by Kimberly Duffy
kimberlyduffy.com

BETHANYHOUSE